RING OF EARTH

Praise for *Ring of Earth*, by William Woolfitt:

Sad and evocative, Woolfitt's collection is reminiscent of early Ron Rash, Breece Pancake, and, at its best, Fred Chappell. *Ring of Earth*'s Appalachian folk struggle on hard yet striking landscapes, go hungry, dream of beach vacations, work in dirty mines, and sleep on shared blankets before fires that are always dying. Women work beside men, give birth to stillborn babies, and cater to partners who hibernate long winters in rooms that reek of despair. And yet, amidst the wreck of land and body, these pieces flare. Despite their lyric hunger and darkness, there is light, if only for a moment.

—Michael Gills, author of
Before All Who Have Ever Seen This Disappear

Woolfitt's language is muscular, fresh, and sharp enough to slice open our vision.

—Cathryn Hankla, author of
Fortune Teller Miracle Fish

I can't stop thinking about this cast of hog farmers, coal miners, country doctors, and children straining against prescribed futures—all of them finely drawn characters who move fitfully against the backdrop of an ailing landscape. Lyrical and deeply moving, these stories are both a paean to the solace we find in nature and a warning against its thoughtless destruction.

—Veronica Montes, author of
Benedicta Takes Wing

RING OF EARTH

William Woolfitt

Lake Dallas, Texas

FIRST EDITION

This is a work of fiction, and is not intended to resemble anyone
living or dead.

Requests for permission to reprint or reuse material
from this work should be sent to:

Permissions
Madville Publishing
PO Box 358
Lake Dallas, TX 75065

Cover Art: Erin Case

Author Photo: Arlyne VanHook

ISBN: 9781956440591 paperback
ISBN: 9781956440607 ebook
Library of Congress Control Number: 2023939885

TABLE OF CONTENTS

WHAT THE
BEECH TREE KNOWS

All that the track-men tip from dumpcarts—rootlets, and clods of dirt, and knuckles of shale—hills up in the July sun. I look out at the tracks while I stand near a beech tree that I know. When I put my hand on its bark, the beech does not quicken or groan. I try to hear its rush of sap, I hold my ear to the trunk, and although I hear nothing, I keep my ear there. At last, I hear a low drumming. But it's only the throb of my blood where my head presses the bark, and even that fades when the trackmen call out a work-song: "on the Red Sea shore, Moses smote the water with a two-by-four."

Too hot to fight the witch-grass and Spanish needles that choke the corn. Flinging my hoe into high thistles, I run into the woods. My aunt will peel a switch; my uncle will vow a beating and track me. I search for rocky overhangs, for certain earth-folds that have concealed me, held me close the way my pocket holds my treasures. An arrowhead, a button from my mother's dress, a curl of her gray hair, the bone dice her father took from the Rebel he shot. I tuck myself into dens, boy-sized wallows in the laurel-hells.

My memories of my parents diminish, are nearly gone from the house where we lived, emptied of their personal goods and bric-a-brac, swept and polished and soaped with lye. I get more of them when I go among the trees they knew, glimpses of my mother gathering leaves and pressing them in her shabby Bible, my father showing me how to make bark rubbings, my mother introducing me to trees almost like they were people. When she sang ballads, she sometimes took out the dukes and the ladies, put in walnuts and birches and willows with their long green tresses. From my parents, I know that hickory is for fires that burn longest. And catalpa tree for bait: my father used the worms that ate the catalpa's seedpods when he fished the Cheat River. Elderberry for the dye my mother called Queen Esther purple. Sourwood for the whistles and spoons that I carve, that my uncle sells in Elkins and Seneca Flats. And woodpeckered beech for watching black crewmen and horse-teams, the tracks at the edge of my father's land. Branch-sprawled, leaf-shaded, I study the ragged stumps that the trackmen leave, and the new bed they smooth, the earth meek and ruled.

Sundays only is there mirth in the house. My uncle and aunt invite the preacher, the elders and their wives, rowdy sons who grapple in the yard. The preacher flashes his big teeth, bangs hymns from my mother's piano that is silent the rest of the week. Between hymns, the preacher takes out his hanky and mops sweat from his forehead, from my mother's ivory keys. When I turn from the piano, I hear an elder say, "He's getting tall." Another says, "Soon he won't be so delicate." My uncle says, "Might work better if there was muscle on his bones." They talk as if I am not there. If they notice me slipping out the door, they give no sign.

Sometimes, I believe that the beech welcomes me, can be companionable, a holder of secrets. That it may greet me with a shiver that I am sure to miss unless I look carefully. Always, the beech offers me a hiding room. And saw-toothed leaves that cool blisters. And branches that I climb to, and spread flat on until I fade from view, as if I am suited in leaves and the smooth gray bark.

For my mother buried under the walnut, my aunt set out a headstone. For my father's tears, his nights of sleeping on her grave, my uncle locked him in the smokehouse. When my father got loose, he roamed the woods in a breechcloth. He said that his Shawnee grandfather visited his dreams, he was going to make a basket from ash splints that could take him to the stars. My uncle sent my father to the Weston asylum.

"When he gets cured," my aunt said, "he'll come back and thank us. We're improving his property, his boy." My uncle claimed my father's acres and house. Now he haggles with the Deer Creek Lumber Company, sells my father's stands of hemlock, spruce, and white oak. My aunt holds a string to me and takes my measure, makes clothes for me, cuts my hair, and busies my idle hands.

Best is the cavity of the beech. There is room for my thoughts here, and old voices, the littlest pieces. My father told me, let the trees show you things. They sent him away the next day. He told me to do the same with a bee gum I was about to rob, a rabbit before shooting it: go soft, go slow. The beech's hollow space is the shape of me if I tuck one arm like a wing, if I stretch the other overhead.

WAX MUSEUM

Jake says that he wishes they could walk along the towpath and scatter bread from the thrift store for the Canada geese. Emerson grabs his neck, squeezes it, and says no way, they're going in the museum to see the dummy get hanged with a noose. They're walking into a café for breakfast. Their mother groans, shakes her head as if she can't believe the things that come out of Emerson's mouth, but then she grins. She tells them that since they've been pinching their pennies, she's got enough for museum tickets.

Emerson is twelve, two years older than Jake. They're away for the weekend, three hours from home, treating themselves to what their father grandly calls a family vacation.

Their mother says mini-getaway: her amused correction, gentle but precise. When she brings their father back to reality, he glares at her.

Each time their father buys something—super-soaker squirt guns, blue raspberry slushies, visors embroidered with "Harper's Ferry" for all four of them—their mother writes it down in her pocket-sized account book, on one of the graph-paper pages where she keeps track of everything. For the last few months, since she started taking a new medicine, she's been bright-eyed, energetic, bossy. Jake likes her this way, acting like her old self, moving through the world with a spring in her step—no longer in a slump, no longer in their darkened living room where she stays on the couch if she's having a bad day.

Jake isn't certain he likes vacations, thinks that too many unpredictable things happen during them. And sure enough, their father was gone without explanation this morning when Jake woke up in the rollaway bed in their musty room at the Hilltop House Hotel. Jake thought maybe his parents had been fighting again and his father had stormed out. Or maybe he'd been abducted. Jake recalled a movie about a shape-changing shadow-alien that stole a man from his house while his family slept.

"Where's Dad?" Jake said. "Where's he gone?"

Emerson ignored him, channel-surfing while winding the drape cord around his thumb, and their mother acted like it was no big deal.

"His bicycle's gone too," she said, painting the arches of her eyebrows. "He gets these whims."

She insisted that they make the beds even though Emerson said let the maid do it. Then she shouldered her boxy purse that reminds Jake of a doctor's bag, full of adhesive bandages, hand sanitizer packets, tissues, coupons, miniature tools, Krazy Glue, all kinds of things. They walked to the café, and now they're sitting at a table beneath a pair of crossed bayonets, eating silver-dollar pancakes.

Jake asks to be excused, using the politeness that pleases his mother, and then he heads to the bathroom. He checks out the back of a man's head that looks like it could be the back of his father's head. The men's room has a sign that says Billy Yank; the ladies' has a sign that says Cotton Belle.

When he returns, Emerson has eaten his last two pancakes. Jake doesn't say anything; he'd rather keep the peace. Their mother is working a crossword puzzle—her favorite thing to do when she's not crocheting squares for a granny afghan. She says that both activities let her put her life in order one box at a time.

Emerson cups his palms under his glass of tomato juice, lifts it over his head, and announces, "I will now drink a tantalizing Bloody Mary."

Their mother shoots him a look.

"If we walk the trail by the river, we might meet up with Dad," says Jake, trying one last time.

"For once, can you just go with the program? Emerson would try to stone the wildlife. I'm in no mood for that," their mother says, waving for the waitress. "And besides, the river is too far when John Brown is right across the street."

"And the hanging," says Emerson. "Don't forget the hanging."

Their mother stations herself on a bench on the sidewalk, takes out her puzzle magazine. She tells Emerson, "Look out for your brother, and be sure you walk him out if he's frightened." She gives the ticket money to Emerson, tells him to put it in his pocket. Then she says to Jake, "You look out for your brother too. If he breaks the rules, if he causes a scene, remind him that I'll hear about it. I always do."

Jake hesitates, but Emerson is already whooping, clamping his meaty hand around Jake's reed-thin wrist; they charge across the street toward a three-story building with thick black paper on the windows. Jake stumbles, does his best to keep up.

The first few rooms of the museum that Emerson rushes Jake through are a blur of bodies and faces. Jake looks at real people, then wax people, then real people again: tourists with headphones on, and a judge in a courtroom banging his gavel, and sunburnt middle-aged ladies in tropical-print culottes, and farmers hacked with broadswords in bleeding Kansas, and squirmy kids who wear the matching neon T-shirts of a summer camp, and wailing farmwives who crouch beside their fallen husbands, and two teenagers holding hands, and free soil men unpacking rifles from just-arrived crates of Bibles. Emerson drags Jake on a chaotic route through the museum—ignoring "Do Not Enter" signs, scrambling under barricades, dashing the wrong way up one staircase, the wrong way down another. Jake tries to tell him he's confusing history, but Emerson doesn't listen.

And then Emerson slows down in a room Jake will not soon forget: a Black boy whimpers as he lifts his arms, tries to block the blows of a white man in a ruffled frockcoat, who's beating him with a shovel. The spotlight shifts to another corner of the room, where the same boy and his father and mother are crying in front of an auction block, reaching for each other, even as white men pull them apart. Jake thinks these white men are even more crudely made than the other wax dummies; their faces look like lumps of putty, and their hands look like meat hooks.

"What if Dad had a bike wreck?" Jake asks Emerson, who has seen enough, is pulling him away from the slavery room. "He's been gone for how many hours? How could that be normal?"

"Or what if he had a flat tire, stopped to fix it, and some fat redneck sheriff thought Dad was a hobo, and threw him in the slammer?" Emerson says.

Emerson slows down again to inspect the train depot room, which at first appears deserted. Emerson presses a green button, activates the player that tells what happened at the depot. He grins at Jake and says, "What if Dad wrecked his bike, and skidded into the river, and drowned, and now the carps are picking his bones?"

If he must be here, Jake would rather read the placard without listening to the hysterics of the creaky recorded voice. "Something terrible is going to happen," Jake says, trying to warn Emerson, who ignores him.

A spotlight floods the platform, where a Black man in a

yellow striped shirt falls on his back and thrashes, while an old white man with a Santa Claus beard crouches alongside him, and opens his mouth to cry out, and wrings his hands. The dying man is the baggage handler, Jake learns, shot while John Brown's raiders sabotaged the telegraph wire, and now his chest inflates as he gasps for oxygen, expands so much Jake thinks it might burst, which would delight Emerson—hunks of wax and fake hair and cloth flying everywhere, raining down on him and Jake. The baggage handler's chest swells, and his breaths rasp like a rusty gate. His chest sinks, and rises, and sinks again.

"This is sick," says Emerson, bobbing his head and puckering his mouth, as if listening to a guitar solo by his favorite death metal band.

Jake can't muster Emerson's enthusiasm. The wax people at the train depot seem too cartoonish, their movements too jerky.

Emerson finds a loose floorboard, manipulates it with his foot to produce a loud groan, uses the groaning floorboard to accentuate the baggage handler's gasps—an effect that Jake hates. Emerson knows a dozen ways to devil small animals, especially if it's Jake's hamster, or his moth that lived for a week in a pickle jar.

The old man with a Santa beard kneels again in the battle-field room, this time haranguing a swordsman while cradling his lifeless son, who's been scored like a pie crust. The narrator-on-tape says that two of John Brown's sons have been killed during the raid.

Some of the sunburnt ladies are also in this room, clustering around the placard, cooling themselves with personal misting fans. The narrator loses half his pronouncements to the cacophony of gunshots, cannon fire, the cries of the raiders and the soldiers, and the squealing horses. Emerson positions himself in the glare of a crimson strobe light that pulses on, and off, and on, so that his head resembles a beet, a parsnip, and again a beet. Chewing gum flies from the mouth of the girl teenager who screams like she's riding a roller coaster. The boy teenager pats her back, massages her arms.

With growing unease, Jake watches the wax people go through their exaggerated motions, the live people overreacting to the carnage, the spectacle. It's like the tight feeling he gets when he studies Emerson and their father watching a football game on TV: Emerson hoots, brandishes his fists, upsets his bowl of chips, and their father grunts when his team returns the kickoff, as if he's straining to lift a heavy weight.

Then the racket and the pulsing lights stop. The girlfriend curls a lock of hair around her pinkie, says "I couldn't take any more of that."

Emerson presses the green button to restart the battle. A sunburnt lady drops her misting fan and tote bag, staggers, falls back, hits her head on the floor. Her tropical shorts ride up, and Jake can see more of her legs than he wants to, big puffy thighs, squiggly purple veins like nightcrawlers.

"Maybe she needs a drink of water," says one of her friends.

The militiaman lifts his saber.

"Call an ambulance!" Emerson shouts.

The old man rebukes his son's attacker again, trembles, holds out his hand. Jake thinks he detects a message here: John Brown wants to do what's right, but it means he loses his family. There's no way he can choose both. He tries to fight slavery, ends up killing the baggage handler even though he's innocent, then sacrificing a son, then two more sons.

The boy teenager hands the girl teenager a pair of bottled waters to free his hands, squats down and checks the crumpled lady's pulse. Her mouth moves, but Jake can't hear her over the thud of the cannon. Her chest heaves like the baggage handler's.

"You okay, little man?" says Emerson. "We can get out of here if you want to go sit with Mom."

Jake has reached a conclusion: the only way to make his world ordinary again, smooth again—a world with a father who doesn't vanish and a mother who would care if he did, with no lumpy rollaway bed in a stale hotel room, no fainting ladies, no dead wax people, no families torn apart and sold to strangers, and no broadswords, no cannons—is to endure the weekend. To heed his mother's request, and give in, and make himself like clay, easy to shape.

"We should check out the gallows. I bet they're insane," he says, copying Emerson's vocabulary and tone. For once, Jake can see some good in encouraging his brother, saying what he wants to hear.

Their father is sitting beside their mother on the bench, holding a honeydew melon on each knee, a plastic shopping bag between his feet. His bike is on its side, blocking part of the sidewalk. The kickstand is broken, but it's just an old secondhand bike; their father could probably fix it, if he ever got around to it.

"I went to buy us a treat at a produce market I remembered," their father explains. "It was boarded up, I saw a man walking his dog, I asked him if the market had relocated. He told me about a place a few miles down a country road." Their father nudges the shopping bag with his foot. Emerson grabs the bag and tears into it.

"Nine miles," says their mother. "Not a few miles."

Their father lets out a long sigh, bites his lip, starts to move his hands, then moves them quickly back to steady the melons on his knees. "Nine miles. Sure, whatever. I don't know how you know that."

The shopping bag tips over. Individually wrapped whoopee

pies and no-bake cookies fall around Emerson's feet. He reaches into the bag, digs around, pulls out a tub of beef jerky, a sleeve of crackers, a package of red candies.

"Who thinks a picnic right here would be fun?" their father says, glancing at their mother. "Did I miss breakfast?"

"Is it okay for people to have picnics on the sidewalk?" says Jake.

"Maybe just this once," their mother says.

"Tell me about General Lee capturing the madman and saving the day," their father says.

"Lee was a traitor," their mother says softly: another gentle correction. "He owned a bunch of slaves."

"Do you have to be right about everything?" Their father jumps up from the bench, turns around and grimaces at all of them. His mouth twitches, his eyes are teary, his face looks crazy. "I get sick of it." The melons have fallen to the sidewalk, are rolling away.

Their mother starts to say something, looks at their father, shrugs, alters the expression on her face. She takes a pocketknife and four plastic spoons from her capacious purse. Emerson says that he'll cut up a melon if they want him to.

Jake tries to do what's expected of him, to act as if everything's fine, as if his parents are the same dependable people they have always been, and nothing about this impromptu picnic seems odd to him. But then he rips open the cellophane package without looking at it first, and shoves a red candy into his mouth, and takes a bite. He almost gags. The candy tastes like crayons, like fruit punch, and his teeth feel greasy, and he spits the candy into his hand. He sees that he's bitten into a pair of wax lips, and the lips look wounded now, and the pink spit from his mouth has already begun to stain his hands.

FIRE SEASON

I was the oldest of five daughters. There was me, then Ethel, and Lilian after her, and lastly the twins. I wanted to carry on the family business, but I couldn't say this to anyone. My daddy was a country doctor and farmer. Much to his grief, he had no sons, and was sure he had nobody with whom he could share his store of knowledge. We had a milk cow, some sow pigs, and chickens. We were a mile from Seneca Flats, the nearest town. I made sure the farm chores were done while he was away on remote house calls, and he had showed me how to roll pills, how to steam dressings, and had taught me a few things about doctoring, about healing. But if I asked too many questions, acted too independently, spoke too freely, he would retreat to his stern opinions about the frailer sex, female vanities, the hen who crows like a rooster and fools no one. *I can do more*, I would always say. This striving had gone on since my mother died—this routine in which Daddy offered me knowledge, and I reached for it, and then he snatched it away. I thought I would never get my chance, that we were set in our ways as surely as mechanical dolls, stubbornly repeating to each other the same tired phrases again and again.

But there came a summer when Daddy went mushroom hunting on Bergoo Mountain and fell ill shortly thereafter. He said he had loved going there when he was a boy. And he wanted me to accompany him; he said he would show me a

grove of spruce trees that likely had bolete mushrooms growing under them. If he and I brought home enough, he said he
wanted Ethel to fix mushroom croquettes and gravy. These
were very old spruces, he said, more than a hundred feet tall.
He told Lilian to keep her eye on the twins while we were gone.

I was pleased to be the one he had chosen for an outdoor
expedition, and eager to learn what he might want to teach
me. That pleasure turned to sorrow when we got to the mountain. There were no mushrooms, no spruce trees. Daddy said,
"Nothing looks the same." He and I followed a twisting path, a
haul road, and then we traced the earth-scars where the logs had
been skidded down Blue Knob to the Cheat River. We passed
through a field of waste, what was left of the trees: slash and
stumps and broken crowns, a few saplings, a mess of brush.
There was a yellow-breasted warbler singing as it hopped on a
jagged log. Daddy and I picked our way around the blast-holes
where the felled poplars, too massive to move, had been shot
with dynamite, then dragged to the skidways.

"Do you know what will happen next?" Daddy said. He
was pale as a sheet.

I said I did not.

"They're going to cut down every red spruce," he said.
"Then the fires will come. When they log all summer, the woods
burn in the fall."

I asked him why they wanted spruce trees.

"Shipping boxes," he said. "Piano frames."

Near the top of the mountain, we knelt on the banks of a clean
stream that Daddy had chosen, and then we lapped its water.

Maybe that water was what gave him the fever. We had
crossed other streams earlier that day that were cloudy, or
choked with sawdust, or stinking of dead fish; we had crossed
a stream dirtied by some fireman who had dumped his train's
ash pan there.

Or maybe Daddy was worn down from overwork, caring for the sick and farming too, going out at all hours of the night, and his strength had run out. Or maybe he had caught some terrible thing from a patient, something too strong for the boiling and soaping and scrubbing he always did. I'm not as certain as I once was.

A few days after we got back from the mountain, Daddy said he had a headache, pain in his back, aching of the bones. He was feverish. He showed me how to use the thermometer again, explained to me the medicine he wanted me to give him. That was on Monday. On Tuesday, I asked him what else would aid in his recovery. He said the best sickroom for him would be sunny, bright, bare. Ethel and I had the sunniest bedroom; at once, I got her to help me move our chifforobe out, take down the curtains, take apart Daddy's bed, put it together in our emptied room.

"I know a bunch of men who would lift the heavy things for us," Ethel said. She gave me a sly grin.

"And you're proud of that?" I said. I didn't think Daddy would like to see Ethel parade her assortment of men through the house. He thought she might be headed for a cheap life.

Ethel didn't bat an eye. "I like a good time," she said.

Daddy told us we shouldn't have gone to so much trouble, but he slept most of the day after we traded rooms. On Thursday, I sponged Daddy and ran a coarse towel over him. His temperature was nearly normal, and I hoped he would be better soon.

Daddy was still sick in bed a couple of weeks after that, and now it was the beginning of September. I had wanted to get him a city doctor from Elkins, but he said that would be too expensive. He said we could send for his old pal Morrison if it came to that, but he was feeling a bit better, he said he thought his sickness wasn't serious. "And I know you'll take good care of me," he said.

Sometimes he had cold sweats. His speech was getting harder for me to understand. One morning, I went in his room to sit with him. I leaned close, touched his brow, and then I worked at sorting out some of the words he sputtered. I tried not to see his brown-furred tongue.

Check it, Suse, he might have said. *Check my bag*. He had a cowhide doctor's bag where he kept a scalpel, forceps, needles threaded with silk and catgut, syringes, a copper pan with folding legs.

"What can I do for you?" I leaned close again. "Is there something you need?"

He didn't reply. His eyelids were twitching. I sat in a chair, waited to see if more words might come. In Daddy's fragments of speech, I wanted to hear that I was the one he had picked, that there were more things he would teach me.

A few minutes later, I was sure I heard him say, *Look in the woods. On the Jamison place, around the old pond, under the cucumber tree*. His tone was more impatient now.

And after that, a wheeze, a croak, something that sounded like, *Radial, ulnar, dorsal*. Then something like *Bee balm, boneset. Oswego tea*.

Or maybe Daddy was muttering, *Be gone soon*. His ragged breath rasped like a saw biting into heart pine. He strained, couldn't sit up, turned his head. I could see that trying to move was painful for him.

What will you do, Suse, Daddy said, and now it sounded like he was accusing me. I saw that his eyes were flinty and cold. *A girl. A girl like you*. And then he let go of the sheet, and his head sank back into the pillow.

Marry or teach, that was what he was getting at, although I had told him and told him that I had no wish for such things.

As if answering him, I got up and did for him what I had done each morning for the last few weeks—things my sisters would not do. I poured him a cup of water and lifted it to his mouth; I tried to get him to eat broth from the spoon I held for him. And then I washed his face and hands; I combed his hair; I changed his clothes, decided that I would try to boil the stench out of them.

While I rubbed his soiled shirt against the washboard, I wondered about his peevishness, his garbled speech. Maybe it meant that he was getting sicker. He had more pink spots on his belly than he did yesterday. His skin was hot. He was light when I lifted him, almost brittle. I thought of milkweed fluff, a dried-out corncob.

When Daddy woke up groaning and it was after midnight, I went to him, touched his cheek, found that he was burning up again. For the first time, I opened his bag, considered the various instruments. At last, I took out the scissors. I cut off Daddy's wavy brown hair, left a few short tufts; I hoped that would ease his fever. "I think you're cooler already," I said, touching his cheek again. He bit his lip, stared at me with his accusing eyes, was quiet until morning.

I kept Daddy's window open day and night so that he could have fresh air, but then I smelled smoke one morning, and then the sky was dark in the middle of the day. There were forest fires just about every year, and they always worried Daddy. I kept his window shut after that.

I asked Ethel about this newest fire. We were washing the supper dishes. She said it was the woods down on Swago Fork. She'd heard that a knot bumper had dropped his cigarette, or maybe sparks had been scattered by a steam locomotive. Ethel liked to talk to men when she had the chance; I could count on her if I wanted to find out what they were gossiping about.

I thanked Ethel for telling me what she knew.

She hung up the dish towel, let out a long sigh, and said, "If you had friends, Suse, you might already know about the fire."

I thought about offering Ethel some sisterly advice; I also thought about snapping back at her. "Do you believe these men you chase around are really your friends? Is that what they're after?" I said.

Ethel's eyes brightened. She loved cutting me down to size. She said, "You'll never have one after you with that dirt on your hands, that flush on your face, that sunburn. Not to mention your strange ideas. Why would any man want a girl who's all burnt up?"

"You need a husband to put you in your place," I said before I could think, the kind of thing Daddy would say. I hated myself for pushing at Ethel the way he pushed me.

Ethel laughed as if I were only teasing her.

I heard Daddy coughing, and I told Ethel I had to go give him a drink of water.

I believed that Daddy was a good doctor. He knew his books, and he knew his plants. When I turned twelve, he had let me read *Poor Man's Friend in the Hours of Affliction*. He'd shown me how to chloroform one of our pigs and stitch it up when it had a wounded leg, how to fit and press together the edges of the gash with my fingers, how to tie the surgeon's knot.

That was about the time he told Lilian and Ethel and me that he had learned the heal-alls from his grandmother Rulina, that she had lived near my aunt and uncle on the Jamison farm when she was too old to live alone. In the winter, she slept in their extra bedroom. But she also had her own summer house, a mud-daubed lean-to built into the hillside where she slept on deerskin in the warm months. She hung ginseng and pinkroot and maidenhair from the rafters, and tied up strings of dried morels, and tended an arbor of fox grapes, and had barrels of sauerkraut and sour corn.

"Maybe I could be an herbalist like Grandmother Rulina," I interjected.

Daddy didn't rebuke me as much as he might have. "She had a hard life," he said. "Don't forget that."

And then he said that when he didn't have so much work to do, he would take us to visit our cousins at the Jamison farm, where he would teach us what common leaves and lowly stems and potent roots we should harvest and keep in our larders. He said Rulina had shown him how to find ingredients for tonics in the spruce forests, where the flying squirrels and speckled salamanders lived. She knew how to find medicinal plants growing in the cool, moist places, among the ferns and liverworts, in the deep drifts of needles on the forest floor.

At the end of September, there were mornings when Daddy seemed stronger, brighter, had some appetite. By noon, he would be weak again. When I insisted, he finally said I could send for Morrison, the doctor over in Winterburn, his friend and rival. Morrison did not reply.

I took care of Daddy, but I was greedy too. I kept hoping he might tell me a little of what I wanted to hear.

There was so much he had not told me. Or so much I had not listened to when he was well. I knew that Daddy was not getting better. I knew that the Jamison place had been bought by the Deer Creek Lumber Company last year. Deer Creek pulled apart the Jamison farmhouse with crowbars, and burned the outbuildings, and then the crews of men came and chopped down the red spruces, the firs, the sugar maples. There might come a day when I would have no choice but to sell Daddy's land to Deer Creek—maybe our woodlots, maybe all of it— but I hoped that I could keep our farm going. If I had to, if I had Lilian and the twins to provide for, maybe I could smooth things over with Ethel. Maybe I would decide to ignore Ethel's mean mouth, and persuade her to marry a man who was good with pigs and plows and long hours in the sun, and she would listen to me for once, and then somehow all of us could make a kind of home together.

If that failed, maybe I could burrow into a hillside like my great-grandmother had done.

I wiped Daddy with wet cloths cooled in the milk-house; poured for him all the water he could drink; steeped pennyroyal leaves from the ravine, made a brew, hoped that it would help him sweat and heave.

He made a terrible face when he sipped the tea. "Ground ivy would be better," he said. "You should know ground ivy."

"Couldn't find any," I said.

"This is for you," he said. "For your schoolroom."

I wanted to protest, to tell him again that teaching was no dream of mine, but I thought I should be patient with him.

He reached under his blanket, handed me a small book with marble paper covers. For a moment, I believed it was his diary. Then I looked through it and saw that most of the pages were blank; a few had anatomical drawings in crayon or chalk.

"You made these," I said.

He smiled a little. "I thought I was a scholar."

I sat by his bed, looked at the drawings with him, described what I saw, got him to comment every so often. I stretched out our conversation for as long as I could. There was an embryo that looked like some trembling wide-eyed creature. There was circulatory man, his veins the branching paths of a treasure map, his heart like a rose, mauve and four-petaled. For his capillaries, my father had used fine brush strokes, as if he were practicing calligraphy. There was skeletal man; his silvery-gold bones reminded me of an armory of shields and pikestaffs and sabers. There was alimentary man, bitten loaf in hand, inside him an array of tubes and pockets and balloons, pillowy and pink.

"The secret workings of man," my father said. I thought he might be about to confide in me, but he was quiet, sinking again, too weak to say more.

I asked my sisters to take turns sitting with Daddy when I went outside to feed the animals or hoe the turnip greens. Lilian sang parlor songs and played the autoharp for him; Ethel and her beau read aloud from Daddy's farming magazine; when we could coax them indoors, the twins linked arms and twirled around his room, or told him what they saw in his window. One twin would point out the shadow of the nearby mountain; the other would say she was looking at nuthatches in the balm-of-Gilead tree, a strip of the prettiest blue sky. That part about the sky was not true; the fire at Swago Fork was still burning, and the sun was dimmed by smoke, and the wind smelled like charred wood.

When I went back inside, Daddy said, "Is he here yet?" I had to remind Daddy again and again that we had sent for Morrison, sent for him more than once, and since that was days ago, surely he would be here soon.

Morrison was redheaded, still strong and handsome despite his age, old-fashioned, clever. He got everyone to laugh, got everyone to love him. He wanted his son Lemuel to become a doctor, but all Lemuel cared about was pig breeds, cream separators, the newest fertilizers. Some of our acquaintances in Seneca Flats preferred Morrison, even though he was not close, even though he still believed in humors and miasmas, in cupping and leeches, or said he did. I thought he was a snake. Ethel said she'd heard that he spent more time in the timber camps than Winterburn; I had a hunch he liked to drink jars of blue ruin with the loggers, and play poker with them, and shoot dice.

While she was taking the wash off the lines, I asked Ethel if her beau knew anything about the Swago Fork fire. She said he thought we were too far from it to be in danger, but it was an awful fire, so hot even the dirt was on fire, even the mud where horses drank. She said he called it the kind *that burns a hole in the sky.*

When Morrison finally came, he said he was hungry, and when I ignored him, he spoke more loudly, asked me for cornbread with warm milk poured on it. While I was in the kitchen fixing a bowl for him, he did his cruel treatments. I heard Daddy wail, and then the thud of something big hitting the floor. I wondered if Daddy had kicked Morrison, knocked him over. I thought I could smell bitter herbs, and vomit, and something like burnt flesh.

I found out later that Morrison put steamed flannel on Daddy's heart, and then he had pressed hot tins against Daddy's feet.

When I brought food to Morrison, Daddy had composed himself, was sitting partway up. "Suse," Daddy said, and for once his words were clear. "Give the doctor my bag. It's for his son. I want a good man to have it."

Morrison and Daddy looked each other in the eye, and then Morrison went to the bed, lifted Daddy's hand, gave it a squeeze.

I was mad at both of them. The bag was right there on

Daddy's bureau; why did he want me to fetch it for Morrison? I thought about throwing it out the window.

After Morrison left, Daddy fell asleep and Ethel came striding in. "If you want to doctor, ask Morrison to teach you," she said. It was like her to see through me and blurt out my hidden wishes, to think all I had to do was reach out and take what I wanted. "He's fond of you. Or I'll ask him, if you're shy. Men like a girl who's friendly and interested."

"Why do you like mocking me?" I was angry at her too. "What if I would rather farm?"

Ethel said, "If it's farming you want, set your sights on Lemuel. He's not out of reach." Then she glanced at Daddy, gave him a long and careful look, and acted like she was surprised by how poorly he was, how sunken and drained. Her shoulders sagged, her face quivered, and for once she had a look of defeat. Daddy was groaning as he tried to breathe. We saw him struggle and twitch, gasping like a landed fish who should be cut from its nets and let go.

During those weeks of fever and fire, Daddy kept his knobby fingers under the sheet, trying to hide from us how they writhed like creatures he couldn't tame. He wasn't eating, would shake his head or apologize if I offered him broth or gruel. Once, I thought he was repeating the word *cherries*. I thought we hadn't canned any last year, but I looked in the cellar anyway. I asked my sisters if they knew anyone with a jar of preserves I could borrow, a tree I could pick a handful from. Ethel must have asked around; she came to me a few days later and said she'd go with me to Slipjohn Mountain, where there was a burnt tract that might still have fire cherries.

To get to Slipjohn, we had to pass near the fire that had started at Swago Fork, had to cross a ridge where we could look down and see the orange tongues of flame devouring the woods below us. There was a clamor of pops and cracks as the spruce trees twisted, groaned, crashed down. Like they were giving up their souls, I thought. The smoke stung my eyes. We came to a cloud of ash that swirled over our path. I would have turned around, but Ethel led me by the hand, swatted the gray flakes that fell near our faces.

When we reached Slipjohn and its burned-over side later that day, I was stunned by how green it was, how changed, how drenched in sunlight. It was awful, but if I didn't think about the fires that had raged here two years ago, I could call it pretty too. There were a few trees that had survived, and although their trunks were charred and blistered, they were leafing again. Fire cherry and blackberry had taken hold as far as the eye could see, devoted their energies to transforming the ruined acres on Slipjohn. Such excess, the glut of pink willow-herb, yellow pilewort, the singsong of bees, such frenzy. I saw some birch saplings poking through. A ground robin called *drink-your-tea*; another was loosening the dirt with its feet, hunting for seeds.

"There's a strange peace here," Ethel said.

Most of the fruit was gone; it was too late in the year, or birds had gotten here first. Ethel and then I tried to reach a few berries that had fattened behind snarls of vine. My sleeves and my hands were pricked. With the thorns scratching messages in my skin, my arms ensnared like that, I was part of the plenty that was still being written.

For the next few days, I sat with Daddy, listened to his pitiful breaths, hoping he would name something else he wanted, something I could give him. But I was also wondering if there would be anything more he could give me. Perhaps a memory of what he and Mama and I were like when I was their only-born, and my sisters were futures away. I listened for whatever stories he might give me, stories that I could take in like a food, so to carry in my body some trace of him.

I didn't get much from Daddy other than the stories he always told. He gave me a little bit about how he met my mother at a pie supper, she had brought a rhubarb pie, his favorite. How he and Mama prayed for a son after I was born. How Ethel, a year younger than me, was born with a heart-shaped birthmark and one eye that did not open, and supposedly those were signs she would be blessed with the gift of special sight. And how two years after that, Lilian was underweight at birth, so tiny she could fit inside Daddy's cupped hands, had to be fed with an eyedropper. How there'd been a boy after Lilian who lived for three days. How the twins, six years younger than me, were born during a hailstorm that knocked all the petals off the apple trees, and would have colicky spells, would get milk-sick, catch the measles.

He didn't like to talk about Mama. She had died after giving birth to the twins. Morrison was there, stitching her where she was torn, and although her bleeding stopped, although Daddy said his work was first-rate, I blamed Morrison. I remembered Mama as hearty, never sick a day in her life, taller than Daddy, her arms muscular and freckled and brown from working all day in the sun with her sleeves rolled up. When she worked at the stove, her face turned red and sweat dripped from her. Her nickname for me was Eight Legs. Her hands were quick and sure when she sharpened her sewing shears, her butcher knife, Daddy's scalpels.

Sometimes, I snapped at Daddy when he offered me his tired old stories, same as always, nothing new that I might sink my teeth into or let dissolve beneath my tongue. I told him to conserve his strength, get some sleep. I could fill in where he left off: Ethel's eye had been just a pucker of flesh until Brother Marsh blew on it and spoke in tongues. And now Ethel was self-assured, fearless, the prettiest by far: Mama had taught her to sew foolish things, and her dresses always had some trick with ribbon, some garnish, and she wore her curly black hair down so that it spilled over her shoulders, and all the boys at church looked at her, only at her. We'd heard that she flirted with the timber wolves who went to Seneca Flats on Saturdays. *She's going to the devil,* my daddy had said. I thought Ethel would get in trouble, but I couldn't stop her.

And Lilian was healthier than ever, black-haired and dark-eyed like Ethel, just as dainty and fine and musical as a chickadee. And sometimes fierce. She rescued baby rabbits from the jaws of the barn cats, and put fallen chicks back in their nests, and tried to save crayfish in glass jars. Her beau was a water-boy for the railroads, a jittery thing whose feelings Ethel had toyed with and trampled on; he was pink-skinned and nervous, too meek to defend himself. Lilian was proud of him, but I thought that he was about as helpless as one of her baby rabbits.

And the twins had rallied from their ailments, after Daddy sang to them and dosed them with onion juice and spruce tea to bust colds and build the blood. Now they frolicked around wild as deer, like the motherless sometimes do. Both of them were fidgety and light-footed, quick to laugh, quick to tell lies.

After losing Mama, Daddy had refused to lose any more of us.

Sometimes, I had been Daddy's helper. Sometimes, he had forgotten I was a girl. Mostly, he thought that I was too willful, too choosy, that I should be practical and marry soon. He had said too many times that if I failed to marry, I could try my hand at teaching school.

Sometimes, I had gone after his knowledge in a roundabout

way, and he would let me assist him. I couldn't say to him outright that I wanted to tend the land and cure the sick. Sometimes, I almost got to be the son he'd never had.

And in his own obstinate way, when Daddy could look from the corner of his eye, when he didn't have to stare straight-on, I think he gave his blessing to what he saw in me. At his bidding, I had rolled bandages and mixed plasters, prepared barley water for the bedbound, and pushed a baked onion through a sieve and given its juice to croupy babies. I pinched the hard-shelled beetles that gnawed his potato plants, and learned to notch the pigs' ears, and when there was a tree he couldn't climb, I wrapped myself around the trunk and hauled myself up into the branches, went high to get him a cluster of waxy red berries.

Morrison came back the next morning and rapped at the door. I could hear him singing to himself, some jaunty little tune.

"My daddy doesn't need you," I said. I was ready to slam the door, lock him out.

"I'm here to look after you," he said in a soothing voice. "You're exhausted. You're depressed. I have a tincture for that; I can give you the first dose." He touched his hat brim, took a step back, and I couldn't decide if his smile was false or charitable.

And Morrison was right: I was tired, and there was nobody else who wanted to do something kind for me, or what might pass for kindness. So I said, "You may visit as a family friend, not a doctor," and let him in, and cooked breakfast for him while he talked to me. He obeyed my wishes, did not mention again the medicine he thought I should take. He chatted about the weather, and about Lemuel, how he was cheery and gentle and steady-handed with farm animals. If he was dropping a hint, suggesting that his son was marriageable, I pretended not to notice.

Morrison changed the subject easily enough. He said that

the Swago Fork fire was consuming another great stand of spruce, and told me a few things about Daddy I had not heard before. "A lumberman was sentenced to hang at Elkins for murder. The populace was invited to watch. Your daddy and I were there, with some doctors and young men who were reading medicine, and a crowd of spectators pressing all around us. After the deputy cut the body down and gave him to us, we brought him that night to Dr. Shinn's house, and put him on a table in a private room. We used up a lot of ice. For days we had his body there, dissecting it. He was laid open. Your daddy said it filled him with awe."

Perhaps Lemuel would offer me his hand. I would decline. I had known him all my life, had talked to him often enough, but I couldn't say what he was like or picture him clearly. Maybe he was medium-sized, solidly built or loosely made, maybe neatly dressed, plain-faced, fair but not pale, light-haired or perhaps balding. He could have been any kind of man.

A few days after Morrison's second visit, I heard Daddy gasp when I washed him. I heard a shallow breath, then an awful silence. And then another weak breath. Daddy's face was hot and gray, a drift of ash.

I didn't need more words from him. That gasp was my inheritance, the little that was mine.

I no longer wondered if Daddy had gotten sick from the stream we drank from, or why the fever struck him and not me. I could see that I was spared for this work, for declining bodies, and for the dead.

*

It was Ethel who handed me the sponge, brought a basin of clean water. "We are sisters," she said. Daddy's bath turned easeful when I whispered *mason jar, spool of thread, locust husk*—the part I tidied after the spilling out, the slow unwinding, the flying away.

Velvet Knob

The hog farmer is grindstone apples, seek-no-furthers, he is primrose balm, sorrel and scuppernong butters, he is carved corn-knife handles and stocking stretchers and tiny mounted soldiers: anything that he can load onto the strawberry roan and sell in the river hamlets, at the crossroads stores.

The hog farmer is the roasting ears his wife blows silk from, shells into the iron wash pot and boils with soda and lye. He is the sorry grains and chaffy kernels, witched butter and good scraps that she sets aside for their hogs because she has a wide, wide love that spreads over their animals too. A sloppy love, a prodigal love. He is the anger that pricks him when he sees his wife on a stroll and thinks she's too carefree, the queasiness that rises in him when he sees that she's dug yellow clay from wheel ruts, yellow clay from the creek-banks where wild ginger grows, yellow clay she will sing over while she forms it into diamonds and birds and moons. He is gladness laced with worry when he sees his wife easing her way home from the creek with a bowl of yellow clay, slow-moving and big with their fourth child.

He is the walleye that slips his boy Spencer's hook, or more likely the walleye that Spencer lets go, tender-hearted and headstrong Spencer who won't learn to hunt and has been known to faint if he sees a drop of blood. He is the persimmon tree his boy Nathaniel can't stay away from, its branches damaged from bending, its unripe fruit that Nathaniel crams into his mouth, eats and eats until he vomits. He is the crooked furrows his boy Malachi plows (the furrows he has to re-plow), the throw-sack of manure Malachi wastes too much of when he scatters it over the hills of corn.

The hog farmer is the desperate gnaw of never enough, of greedy hands that grab and hold tight, of his tired and aching body that must always work more. He is the fear that his boys will stay stuck in their troublesome ways, no matter how he tries to train them, bridle them, the fear that they will not grow. He is the dream of snake in the chicken house, blackbirds in the corn, fire in the hay barn.

His wife is bread cast upon the waters, she is salt-rising dough and angel flake biscuits she gives away. She is the rafters and the pie safe and the root cellar that store the things she hands to anyone in need. She is a string of leather apples, a bag of shucked beans, a platter, a burlap sack she's happy to share. She is a plain cotton dress dyed in pokeweed tea.

When the baby in her belly kicks her ribs, she takes a deep breath, and she is the calm green waters of a still pond that's receding each year. She's past forty, thought her childbearing years were far behind her, and she feels like a strange miracle has made itself in her body, has nested there. Sometimes she shudders at the mystery of it, sometimes she laughs.

When old Lacy Anne Boggs shouts through the window, asking to borrow a cup of flour, she gives her a two-pound sack.

The hog farmer is thirty acres on the ridge above Ivydale and Morocco, he is the gravel lane, the ruts. He is the rocky hill field in the shadow of Velvet Knob. He is the creek that tumbles through the woods, and meanders, and feeds the Elk River.

He is the chicken coop, the speckled eggs, he is Berkshire hogs rooting in the woods. He is the pierced neck vein, the scalding place, the gambling stick. He is shoulders and middlings and legs that he salts in the meat box and hangs in the smokehouse in March, he is sausage meat packed in corn shucks and white cloth sacks. He is the cornfield, the garden, two kinds of potatoes: Irish and sweet.

When a raggedy man comes to the door selling apple trees, the hog farmer's wife gives him dinner the hog farmer hasn't eaten yet. When she sees his trembling hands, the shiver of his goose-pimpled arms, she gives him the hog farmer's shirt, his hat, a pair of his shoes. A tramp, the hog farmer will call him. She is give until it's foolish, give until it hurts.

She is the peace she speaks to the hog farmer when he simmers, when he boils over, when he scolds her for her reckless charity, when he balls up his hand to strike a foolish son.

She is the Bible stories she reads to discipline her sons when they disobey, or fight, or tell lies. She is her promise that she'll never whip again, never soap a mouth again. She is the words that hush her boys, scare them, awe them, turn them around. She is parable and proverb, she is dust of the ground and the small still voice, she is frogs and gnats and river of blood.

The hog farmer is the forked peach stick or the wire bent into the letter y that he holds with both hands when he dowses for more water, for a new well to dig, when he walks his fields, crisscrossing wagon paths and hog paths with his arms stretched out. He is the twitching of the stick or the wire when he passes over a vein of water, the twitching that spreads to his arms and the thrum that pulses through his body.

He is the creases of his farm, the limestone cliff his boys slide down, the boulders with tatters of lichen, the sinkhole that he shovels dirt into and cannot fill, the blackberry thicket, the holler where the Moccasin Rangers bound his uncle to a hemlock tree and shot him to death. His uncle was named Malachi, and the hog farmer's daguerreotype of him shows a man with fierce eyes, a jutting nose, a proud chin. He is remembered as industrious and god-fearing, a chair maker, a toy carver. So far, the hog farmer's son Malachi is lazy, clumsy with knives, not much like his namesake uncle.

The hog farmer is the ledge over the pool in the creek where Nathaniel and Malachi and Spencer laze around when the sun is fierce and bright, he is the glittering pool of minnows his boys splash in. It was his wife who told the boys about the pool when they said it was too hot to work, who put ideas in their heads, got them thinking about its cool waters. His boys who steal his tobacco and papers, who forsake their chores if he doesn't watch them and drive them hard, his boys who shriek like blue jays and strip off their clothes and paint yellow stripes on their faces and chests.

The hog farmer's wife is the ragweed that she chews and smears on Nathaniel's bee stings, the puffy welts on his face and neck. She is the cool yellow clay she applies to Nathaniel after that, greedy Nathaniel who throws rocks to bring down bees' nests because he loves honey. Nathaniel who has a crow's eye for whatever's flashy or sparkling, and a mosquito's whine when he doesn't get what he wants, and a bear's taste for things sickly sweet. Nathaniel who is their nephew, who has lived with them at her invitation since his parents' marriage fell apart, whom she loves as surely as she loves her own sons. Even when Nathaniel slips off to the Hartland coal camp and takes part in the muzzle-loader contests and drinks corn liquor there, competing with miners and wild boys, when nobody knows where he is or even if he will come home, she claims him completely, prays that angels gather around him, that nothing scorches him, that nothing swallows him, and she names him *our son, our son.*

When her hands are calloused, briar-pricked, work-sore, she is the clay she presses her palms in, then her fingers, the backs of her hands.

When his wife feels faint, has pains, when she feels the baby fluttering like a bird, when she stays near their low wooden house, the hog farmer is sumac berries and pigweed, shepherd's purse and sow thistle that he pulls up for her and sets aside from the garden, from the acres he's trying to clear. He is purslane leaves that she crunches with her strong teeth.

He burns the broom sedge field, he ashes the garden, he tries to weed the rocky hill field and pry up every last rock, he tries to tear out sumac brush and rambler rose with a briar hook. He thinks his working of the land might show that he loves it; he worries her eating of the land might show that she wants to become it.

The hog farmer's younger brother entered into that unfortunate marriage, and he moved away from the ridge below Velvet Knob, and he worked the hoot-owl shift in a coal mine that shorted his pay, had him digging in small light, in bad air that made his lungs rattle, in cramped rooms with dirty water everywhere. The younger brother and his wife lived in a Jenny Lind house in the Blue Eagle coal camp with Nathaniel, who was still their little boy.

The hog farmer's wife is the Jacob's ladder quilts she gave to them, although the hog farmer tried to stop her, and the cornmeal, the jar of honey, the tub of sauerkraut, and the hams. When his brother's wife screamed at his brother for tracking in coal dust, threw their plates at the wall and broke them, the hog farmer's wife is the china set she packed up for them.

"We'll eat on tin," she told the hog farmer.

"But I got you those little cups and saucers with pink roses," he said, and she would remember her surprise at the poor-me whimper coming from his mouth.

"I'll drink from the dipper," she told the hog farmer, and then she put her mouth on his fingertips. "I'll drink from your hands."

The hog farmer is the ash heap by the garden that Malachi stumbles into on the morning of the first day of school, or maybe Nathaniel pushed him into it, Malachi won't say. The hog farmer is Malachi's smudgy face and streaky arms when he's too busy to fetch water and boil a tub and get out clean clothes for hapless Malachi, Malachi who is all thumbs and two left feet, who is big and strong for his age but ungainly, who dulls knife-blades and breaks shovel handles no matter how many times the hog farmer tries to teach him their proper use.

And who will look after the dirty boy? Where is his wife, who is surely too pregnant to have gone far? What will she give away today? How will she absolve Nathaniel this time? Anger churns in him. She's at the creek, he guesses. At the creek, cooling her swollen feet, chewing wild ginger, patting a loaf of clay. At the birch, the sassafras, tasting bark, tasting leaves.

The hog farmer's wife is man-of-the-earth that she discovers when she digs morning glories in the gully, its roots shaped like a person's leg, the biggest ones that she drags home, must be twenty pounds each, tasting something like a wild potato when she cooks them—but her boys push their plates away, want no part.

She is the song that she likes to sing while she washes clothes, the one about Scotland town, a far country, the man who dresses in a beggar's rig so he can spy on his untrue love, so he can put his ring in her glass of wine. She is the *Kentucky Harmony* tune book, the shape notes she sings at brush meetings.

She is the apple box she sits on in the dooryard after dark, she is three or four stars she sees when the clouds pull apart, the silver light as she sits there listening to her husband's hound rove and yip, giving song to things distant and unseen.

The hog farmer is the saw briars and blackjacks and scrub pines that spring up faster than he can clear them from the rocky hill field. He is honey in the crock that his wife hides from him, that he sneaks his finger into when he wants to steal a lick. He is the sins he won't name and likes too much to quit. He is skull cracker, panther's breath that burns his throat, makes his eyes drip, sours his stomach.

The hog farmer's wife is the morning that she spends talking with the Syrian peddler, the afternoon, the whole day. She meets him while she's digging blue cohosh along the gravel lane, and she sits with him in the shade. She watches him slip off his canvas straps, watches him unpack his box, and then his valise, and then his notions case. He tries to sell her hand-mirrors, cotton checks and ginghams, papers of sewing needles, cards of horn-buttons and lace, wart removers and dandruff cures and hair food. He tells her that he's carried his box through Cheat country, the spruce woods there, that he's traveled down the Monongahela River on a skiff. She asks him to tell her more. Sometimes he runs out of English, and then they speak to each other by wriggling their fingers and making shapes with their hands.

She is a few silver coins tied up in a handkerchief that her husband doesn't know about. The peddler tells her he misses his village on a mountain, the terraces, the young cedars, the goat herds, the Maronite church with its iron steeple. She buys a prayer book and a saint carved from olive wood and painted Jerusalem gold—a holy woman that she can hide in her apron—and then she presses her remaining coins into the peddler's hands. Another gift. He tells her that even on a still day he hears the wind singing when he stands among the great spruces, hears the branches stirring, and it sounds like the waves of the sea.

The hog farmer tells his wife she can't keep giving her best to anyone she meets, it's selfish of her, she's gone too far this time—but then she reaches for him. He is his wife's arms when she clutches him, he is the wings of her shoulder blades when she turns from him. Her voice and dreams are the only gold he knows, he is the gold of her, the gold of sundown and Elberta peaches and poplar leaves and moss that grows between roof-shakes, he is gold in her hands. He is motes of hay in barn light, grass-bits caught in a ray, in a spill of gold that spears through the cracked gray boards. He is cedar smell, and the soft bed, and the odor of wood-smoke caught inside his house.

"Have a moon," she says, offering him a crescent she's formed.

Clay on her tongue, on his lips, he is the taste of earth on her hands.

Sons with Apples in Their Hands

Nicolo copies his father when he doesn't know what else to do. When his father sits down for breakfast and blows on his hands, he sits and blows too. The front room of the hut is dark and cold, even when his mother tries to build a fire that will warm all of them, even when she creeps out at night and steals the little coal that the trains might have spilled, or finds bits of coal in the burning gob pile at the edge of the camp. She gives them hot porridge. From the bowl to the sop-bread to his mouth, Nicolo doesn't smell or taste it, though his mother added something, might be specks of nutmeg. The bread is coarse and gritty, no color, no taste.

His mother waters and crumbs the porridge for the breakfast of his brothers, who will sleep another hour, then rise for school. She waits at the door with his father's dinner pail for him to carry. He will share the pail until they can buy him his own. The only thing darker than the sky behind her will be the underground rooms that eat all their hours, the rooms they hollow and enlarge and prop up with puny timbers. He doesn't check the sky for signs of sunrise anymore, ribbons and streaks of pink and pearl. His mother gets up before them to pack their lunch, goes to bed after them too, stays up sewing in the dark. *I don't see too good*, she sometimes says. *I got weak eyes.* She sews by the feel of seam, the prick of needle, the tug of thread.

Sparrow-faced and jittery, his mother peeps at them, averts her eyes, peeps again, worries the wipe-rag, clutches it with both hands. His father kisses her cheek, and then Nicolo copies, kisses her cheek too. Kissing her cheek is like kissing bone.

She slips something into Nicolo's hand. An apple with wrinkly skin, the size of an egg, the dull red of an old bruise.

He refuses, says that his father eats more.

"I want my boy to have it," she says.

"Alberto has school today."

"I got one for him too." She presses his brow with the back of her hand, as if checking for fever. "I know your face now," she says. "If I keep part of you with me, the rest will come back to me at the end of the day."

Here's the mud road, frozen into ripples and crests. Nicolo tries not to stumble. In some yards, the earth is bare, packed down and wind-scoured; the grass in other yards is chewed to nubs, too short to move with the wind.

Nicolo's grandfather, uncle, and cousin emerge from the nearby huts. His cousin Marco is a year older, two inches taller, bulky and strong; Marco loads his own wagon, carries his own tag, draws his own pay. Marco barely lifts his feet, his head drooping, his eyes almost shut, saving his strength, won't come alive till they go underground.

"Feels like a big snow is gonna bury us," Nicolo's uncle tells him. His uncle likes to comment on the weather, foretell a warming or a cooling, a snow that blankets, a wind that strips. His uncle licks a finger, holds it aloft; for further clues, he reads the swelling of his knees, the stripes of caterpillars, the angles and circumferences of icicles.

Nicolo doesn't know what he should say to his cheery

uncle. He doesn't want snow, or colder days, or things that could cover him, pile on him.

"Snow would be a mercy," his grandfather says. "Change everything, make your mother happy, something pretty to look at." He carries in his dinner pail a charred madonna and a flask. The madonna is a branch-scrap who revealed herself to him in the remains of a fire. At lunch, his grandfather will take her from her blue flannel wrapping and nest his hands around her, or drink from the flask, or both. *In case one don't warm these old bones,* he sometimes says. His grandfather made Nicolo hold her once. She was bigger than his hand, but she weighed almost nothing, had all the wood-sap burned out of her. She was kneeling. He could identify two feet, hands joined for prayer, lumpy nose, grooved mouth—but she had no eyes, not even eyeholes. His grandfather said, "Pray if you want to." She was burnt, and maybe she had been forced to kneel and clasp her hands, like a captured soldier. He handed the madonna back to his grandfather so fast he almost dropped her.

When he was eleven, Nicolo still went to school in the basement of Our Lady of Consolation, where he exchanged notes with Charlotte. His classroom was crowded and dim, smelled like chalk and the slimy brown soap Miss Underwood made them wash their hands with, like the frozen wool socks and the thawing shoes that puddled the floor. In the winter, Miss Underwood dismissed them early if they ran out of lamp oil. A boy might quit school when he was too big to share a desk, or sooner, if his father wanted him, had decided to take him into the mine. Charlotte was two years older, and a head taller, but there were no boys her age. Nicolo's notes contained mostly pictures. He was bad at spelling. He drew flying dragons, hunchbacks, elephants, wise men riding camels, men thrown into a great coke oven and dancing in a fire that did not consume them, all the people in the stories his mother told as he and his brothers fell asleep at night. Charlotte wrote sentimental poems for him, the loops and tails of her cursive letters blossoming into leaves or vines or arrow-pierced hearts. Miss Underwood never caught Charlotte. Her notes appeared, as if by magic, inside his copybook or his shirtsleeve. Charlotte had the hands of a thief.

Marco scuffs his feet; his uncle recites his suspicion of snow to the other men they meet; his grandfather hacks like a drowning man, coughs a wet gurgling cough, spits, starts all over again. His father moves into the day without a sound. Then Marco and his uncle turn at the fork in the road that leads to the number seven hole. His grandfather squeezes Nicolo's bicep and says, "I wish I had a strong boy like you to help me load. You tell Alberto to come work for me before all those books swell up his head."

His grandfather leans down and kisses the top of his head, then turns toward number seven. He and his father cross the slab bridge over the West Fork of the Monongahela, and continue walking to number five. They line up behind other men, stomp and shift to stay warm, exhale into their cupped hands. Then it is their turn. The boss checks his father's name, gives each of them a carbolic lamp, and gives his father his tag, a paper cone of powder, and fuses. The manager jots in his ledger whatever he doles out, subtracts it from his father's pay.

They enter the mouth of the hole, the fuzzy half-dark that awaits them just past the mouth. They climb into the middle car of the mantrip, stand among the other men, their bodies close enough to share heat.

At twelve, Nicolo went to work in the breaker room, along with twenty other boys and a few old men too feeble to work underground. The floor was slanted, and the clattering coal streamed past them. Full wagons were dumped at the uphill side of the room; empty wagons at the downhill side caught the sorted coal. He had to pick out slate, sometimes a clump of earth or a stick. He had to be quick, or the chunks would mash his fingers. An overseer watched them, would strike a boy if he let slate get past him.

The discarded slate was driven to the gob pile, which was always burning, and then it was dumped there. Nicolo thought the smoke smelled like rotten eggs, had seen the smoke-blackened huts of the families who lived near the gob pile.

A strange boy named Silvio joined them. He wore a floppy hat that shadowed his eyes. He chuckled when nothing funny had happened, clamped fingers over his mouth, laughed and snorted into his hand. His first week, he worked beside Nicolo, and they made a game of piling the slate into towers, seeing who could make his the highest. Once, each of them found a fossil—whorl of snail, ghost of fern—and after much haggling, decided they would trade. When one of the bigger boys kicked Silvio, Nicolo kicked the bigger boy. The overseer kicked both of them, said they were too big for the breaker room. Time for them to work underground.

"We got a real good mine," his father told him. "Big rooms, dry rooms. I don't have to crouch or work in water. Not much dust, not much gas."

"You won't have to be down there long," his mother told him.

Nicolo was tired of getting his fingers bruised in the breaker room, tired of the blue spots under his fingernails. He told himself he was ready for the mine.

He flings another shovelful into the wagon. When rock hits rock, dust rises in plumes and coils. He flinches, cups his hand over his mouth and nose, counts to five. He feels the apple in his pocket. No chance to eat it secretly. His father mutters at him, knows that he slowpokes. His father never slows down, never stops watching him. He tries to imitate his father's steady rhythm. He turns and angles his head so that the long skinny worm of light from his carbolic lamp parallels the light from his father's. He stoops when his father stoops, jabs his shovel into the drift of shattered rock at his feet, strains to lift it to chest-level.

At thirteen, Nicolo worked as a trapper, his first underground job, stationed in the tunnel at a heavy wooden door. He shouldered it open to let the horse-drawn wagons pass through, grabbed its steel ring with both hands and dragged it shut to capture the sweet surface air that the giant fan blew in. Without the fan, without trapper boys to capture the breathable air, all the rooms would fill with stink damp. And black damp that could suffocate the men and the horses and the rats. And fire damp that could blow them up at the touch of even the littlest spark. Nicolo chalked pictures on the door with a nub of slate: pirates and jousting knights, crocodiles and hot air balloons.

The company idled the men a hundred days that year. In the summer, when Nicolo was idled and Alberto was out of school, they tried to fish the Monongahela with sapling poles and the halved bodies of tomato worms from their mother's garden, with hooks and lines from the company store. Nicolo enjoyed flinging the hook as far as he could, using the muscles of his back and arms for a different sort of exertion. They didn't catch anything. Alberto said they should look for pictures in the clouds, maybe they would see a fish there. He was a hopeful boy. Nicolo was watching the river. Scabs of oil rainbowed the water; cinders from the coke ovens swirled in the currents.

His fingers crack and bleed. His bones throb. Dust furs his eyebrows. And dust gets into his mouth, nose, and eyes, staining his spit and snot and tears. A month and a day he has been a man, hand-loading as the men do. Or pretending to hand-load. His ears fill with the coughs and curses of men laboring in the honeycomb of rooms. The snorts, whinnies, and hoof-steps of horses. The boom of fired shots. Clang of shovel-work and pick-work. All these stick inside his head, pound and pound when he tries to sleep in the nest of blankets and brothers in the back room of the hut.

His nose understands the oldness of the earth, how every dead thing keeps rotting and crumbling in its grave or its dying-spot, how the dust of the dead sinks down and down. That ancient smell, mingled with the sweat and urine and excrement of horses and men. His eyes gnaw on the darkness, hungry for color, or shape, or light. He coughs up strings of phlegm. His eyes boil over with hot bitter tears. He plants his shovel in the earth, leans against the chilly tunnel wall, and then he escapes.

He dreams an island of golden sand. A boy who looks like him tows a small boat. The boat almost sinks from all the horse mackerels and red snappers the dream-boy nets for his mother. The scales of the fish are iridescent. The waves lap around his calves.

At fourteen, Nicolo tended the mine horses in the underground stable. He watered them; he fed them oats, linseed, and sugar beets. He mucked their stalls and oiled their collars, curried the thick dust from their bodies, and tried to scrape loose the stockings of mud that clung to their legs. He scoured the soot from the glass panes of the lanterns. The men and boys who worked in the barn needed all the light they could get. The horses wore leather bonnets to protect their heads from low roofs, were shod with double-thick shoes because they never got to walk on soft ground. Everyone said they were sun-starved and blind because they had lived underground for so many years.

"They live better than us," his father said. "They get good food, all I get is thistle coffee and shoes patched with cardboard."

"Because men are cheaper than horses," his grandfather said.

Lunch break, hunkering in a quiet circle in the lunch hole near the main haulage-way, Nicolo and his father congregate with neighbors, another uncle, men who attend Our Lady of Consolation. Chirping rats scamper between their feet, scavenging the scraps. The tail of a rat whips his bare ankle. Chicory coffee in the bottom half of the dinner pail, sandwiches in the top. For him and his father, half a fried egg might be the only filling, or butter, or a smear of meat grease—but his mother always finds something, stretches, invents, never sends them with plain bread.

Polish men form a boisterous circle nearby, joking and bragging, he guesses from their tone. They switch between Polish, which he doesn't speak, and English so twisted that he can't sort it out. He thinks he catches a few names: Kuba, Lew, Albin. They eat double-fisted, tear a mouthful from the loaf in the right hand, another from the lump of bacon in the left.

Three Black men, too few for a circle, squat against the wall. Their lunches vary—a chicken baked whole one day, boiled turnips the next, boiled eggs. Some days, nothing.

His father's lamp goes out. The men hand it around, shake

or thump it. A Black man comes over, says his name is Levi, tells his father he might be able to fix the lamp.

Nicolo studies the other two Black miners. They are eating nothing today. One is fisting and unfisting his hands—a scrawny boy in oversized clothes, cuffs rolled up. The third man dozes. Nicolo can't see much else.

He has already bitten into his sandwich. He goes over to the boy and says, "How come you got nothing to eat?"

"The same how-come that brought me down here against the counsel whispered to me by the Holy Ghost," the boy says. "My brother made me. Ma's going to be mad at him."

He says, "This your first day?"

"And my last, I fervently hope. Even Jesus only had to spend three days descended into hell preaching unto the spirits in prison."

"You want some sandwich? You want to tell me your name?"

The word *sandwich* makes the boy bite his lip. He says, "I definitely do. Even Elijah had the ravens bring unto him bread and flesh when he hid by the brook Cherith, according to the word of the Lord."

The boy holds out his hand.

Nicolo puts the sandwich behind his back. "Say your name first."

"I'm Ebenezer," the boy says. "Folks call me Eb, if that gets to be too big a mouthful."

He wants to know more. He says, "Where you from?"

Eb says, "Somewhere you don't know. The South."

He tears the bread. He says, "What part?"

"My brothers and I were born in Tallapoosa, Alabama. Ma's back there in Goldville."

He offers Eb the unbitten half. Eb glances at the dozing man, then pops the half into his mouth. His cheeks bulge. He gobbles the bread like the starving might do.

The light of his father's lamp brushes the back of Nicolo's neck. Levi calls, "That's enough preaching, Eb."

Nicolo turns around, sees his father and Levi laugh, shake hands. He roots his hand into his pocket, grips the apple. Tomorrow, he tells himself. If Eb must come for another day of work, if Nicolo meets up with Eb, then he'll give Eb the apple. Why give it to someone he won't see again, someone who claims he's about to get free of the mine? Nicolo holds onto the apple, squeezes like it's the last good thing he'll ever be given. Greed may be foul like stink damp, greed may taste like marrow and copper pennies as it coats the roof of his mouth, but he tells himself it has no part of him, greed has no hold.

Nicolo dreams his mother gives him a bouquet of crimson and purple carnations that he gives to a girl he loves. Then he is back in the sea, floating on his back, and Charlotte swims to him, her reddish-brown hair streaming around her shoulders. She teases him, splashes water in his face. He shows her how to dive for little white shells, snail shells, mother of pearl shells, too many for their hands to carry—and they stay down too long, and with lungs burning, they flail back to the surface.

Nicolo's father shakes his arm, and he coughs. The little white shells turn to bits of coal, and it's the bad air of the mine that hurts his lungs, not the ocean. His dream vanishes, snuffed like candle flame. He jerks away, stumbles into the tunnel wall. His father is a hard, knobby man, eternally squinting, bad circulation, no pink in his lips or fingers, even if he cleans them. He has slits for eyes, crabapple cheeks.

Nicolo wishes that he could escape another way, one that would please his father. That he could make himself unthinking, unhoping, dreamless, nothing but a body, a body that digs, and lifts, and throws coal into the wagon, too intent on his work to notice monotony, or pain, or the passing of time. That he could will himself to become a coal boy, a slate boy—that hard, that unfeeling.

"Nicolo! Come sweep up the dust, then I will show you how to bore the hole. And light the fuse."

His fingers are frozen, or stiff, or stupid. They uncurl so slowly from the handle of the shovel, like the taproots of some tired old tree.

The driver brings a horse, ties it to their brimming wagon, and takes it away. His father wheezes while he sweeps the endless dust from their room.

"Good enough," his father says, putting on the breastplate and the auger that makes him look like a man impaled. "Good enough." He drills holes in the face of coal at the back of the room, bearing down on the auger with the weight of his body. His father gives him the cone of powder, and tells him to fill the holes. His father inserts the fuses, uses the tamping stick to pack each hole with the clay he carries in his pants pocket. He fusses over the holes, jabs the clay, lathes away the excess like a baker frosting a cake.

"You got to seal the holes real good," his father says. "You don't do that, you'll set your coal face on fire."

Nicolo runs his fingers over the face, the fuses coarse, the coal smooth, the clay plugs a different kind of smooth.

"Fire in the hole!" his father shouts, though the two of them are alone in the room. "You run for it, and I'll come after. When I say five, get down on your knees and hide your eyes."

The boom deafens him, feels like hot pokers rammed into his ears. His teeth tremble. The ceiling and the walls vibrate like an iron bell bashed by a cannonball. The vibrations devil the dust and grit, churn it into a cloud that seethes from the room behind them. For once, his father stops working, watches with his mouth agape, body frozen. His father pauses a moment, another moment, and then they return to the crop of fragmented rock, the fresh tons they will load.

Someday, the earth will fall on them. He knows it. A hiccup, a sneeze, a burp, and he will be crushed like mustard seed in a pestle, his bones pulverized. No fossils to mark the passing of his life. Nothing left of him but the dust of the dead.

Soup for supper. His mother makes him wash his face and hands again. He doesn't argue. If he did, she would say, *so you'll know how to clean up and look nice for when you get a better job. When you don't go underground anymore.*

His father eats with grime around his eyes, packed under his fingernails. His mother can't make his father do anything he doesn't want to do.

In the back room, he and Alberto and their three little brothers spread the blankets by the warm wall that has the cook-stove on the other side of it. He tells his littlest brother to sleep by the wall, and makes Alberto take a spot in the middle, and gives himself the cold outer spot.

Alberto says, "You want my apple, Nicolo? I wanted to give it to somebody, but I never got a good chance."

He says, "Was it a girl? You got your eye on somebody?"

Alberto giggles.

"Probably that dumb old teacher," a little brother says.

Their mother comes in and speaks to them stories about the dancing water and the bird who talks night and day, about the man wearing purple and fine linen who locks his gate, the beggar who wakes up in Abraham's bosom. She holds the book close, her nose almost touching the page. When she leaves them, he is the only one awake. The brother between him and Alberto turns over, curls against him. Two blankets, and five brothers, and night is the time for their bones to grow strong. For dreams to fill them with things that are beautiful, and melodious, and soft, and fragrant, and savory.

CROW STORIES

I've heard the Crow stories so many times I remember them better than some of my own memories. They were my bedtime, naptime, and story-time stories; now they mix with the stories about my parents I tell myself when I put together the pieces of them that come back to me.

I think my parents told Crow stories to each other too, in whispers, in each other's arms, silvered by moon-stripes coming in through the blinds. The stories were their chance to marvel at something, to grab and hold it close. And maybe the stories were their way of saying to each other *I'm sorry* and *I didn't mean that* and *I'll try*. They finished each other's sentences because the stories had become familiar, and easeful, and calming, a litany each of them said many times.

When my parents were young and fine-looking and not yet hunched over, not yet scarred, they lived for a time in a small cinderblock house in Hercules, one of the chemical towns that had sprung up in the Kanawha Valley. There was a storm the night my parents drove me home from Charleston Memorial Hospital. I was a few days old. My father thought that the rain was too fast for the windshield wipers, and he pulled over three times. My mother told him that she knew how to look past the rain, that he should let her drive. He told her he didn't believe her, and so she sat in the backseat and held me the whole way.

When we got home, we had to wait almost an hour for the rain to die down. My father found a station he liked on the radio, and while Patsy Cline sang her song about love making you do crazy things, he climbed into the back to be with my mother and me. My mother fell asleep, and dreamed that the dirty river that ran through the valley had flooded, and that the three of us were safe inside a giant floating bathtub.

Later that night, the pin oak tree in our front yard came crashing down. My father thought that wind had toppled it; watching from her bungalow across the street, Mrs. Yamato claimed that she had seen tongues of lightning hit the pin oak. It just missed our house. One branch scratched our window. Crows spent the night on our front porch, their nests in the pin oak ruined.

Mrs. Yamato saw the crows hopping on our porch the next morning. She screamed and threw down her chopsticks. An omen of death, she thought. She picked up a broom and came running over. All the crows flew away, except a baby. My father put the baby crow in a shoebox and thanked Mrs. Yamato for her concern. My mother went into the yard, walked around the fallen pin oak and its jagged stump, poked into the fallen nests and found shiny things: beer tabs, bottle caps, electrical wires, bits of tinfoil, an old pair of glasses, Father's screwdriver, her own gold pendant necklace.

My father asked my mother for old rags; he wanted to make a nest for the baby crow.

"Don't tell me you're keeping that bird," she said sternly. "Don't think for a minute that I'll take care of it."

"Crows fly away at six weeks," he said. "Trust me."

This is how it was in our town: Mother kept the windows closed because the air smelled like varnish and burnt mustard. She learned to ignore the scream of the emergency whistle, the sulfurous clouds of smoke, the leaks and spills and fumes. Our house was perched on a hill above the factories that made rayon and pencil lead and assorted chemicals, above the railroad tracks and the dirty river. Once, there had been salt springs in the riverbanks, and Indians had boiled kettles of brine. Long before that, there had been a great sea.

My father worked at one of the chemical factories, at first in the weedkiller division. All the newly hired men started out in weedkiller, got reassigned after a year or two if they proved their mettle. He was part of a crew that stirred the weedkiller ingredients together, let the mixture dry into powdery blocks and then packed the hardened blocks into bags. At the end of the day, there was the problem of what to do with the waste powder that was all over the floor, the machines, stuck to the workers' clothes and hair. My father burned it in a boiler or took a hose and washed it into the storm drains. If the boss liked you, he would send you to dump a truckload of powder in the woods in Putnam County. My father was not among the favorites; he complained too much about the red patches that became blisters on his face, about the rash on his hands. The foreman gave him a tube of cream for the rash—useless, my father said.

For a time, my mother tried to ignore his complaints. Before I was born, she was a part-time bookkeeper at the chemical factory where my father worked. Wanting to be a legal secretary and live in a big city, she was slowly accumulating a wardrobe that she meant to save for that future: black suits, pale blouses. It would be one more way to distance herself from the rough farm of her childhood, near Handley, in the upper part of the valley. She and my father had honeymooned at Niagara Falls, and she had a snow globe from there that she shook and stared into when she wished she was traveling again. On Saturdays, while my father tinkered with motorcycle parts in the ramshackle shed behind our house, she went to matinees at the

Lyric Theater and forgot about the factory. In the flickering light of the movie, on her plush seat, she could be dreamy, carefree, a fugitive from her life.

We all slept in the same room, I in my bassinette, Crow in his shoebox, my parents in their brass bed. Crow hated to hear me crying, and he plucked at his feathers before he learned to hum lullabies. My mother would have objected to any pet my father brought into the home, but then she woke up one night because I was crying. She waited to see if I would quit crying on my own, or if she should get up and check on me. Then she heard strange music, a raspy squawk. It was Crow mimicking the melody of my favorite song, Itsy Bitsy Spider.

It was not the last time Crow changed her mind.

My father fed Crow three times a day. Before work, after work, and an hour before bedtime. He knew he would anger my mother if he spent money on things she considered a luxury, but he went ahead and ordered calcium supplements and vitamins from a catalog. He mixed oatmeal and boiled egg yolk and ground beef heart, globbed it onto his finger, stuck his finger into Crow's throat to make him swallow.

Sometimes, my mother fed me at the same time.

Crow did fly at six weeks, but not away. My mother went to the hardware store, brought home a cage for Crow to roost in at night. In the day, Crow pecked the door if he wanted out, the doorbell if he wanted in. He learned to talk before me. His first words were *in, out, food, sky, crow, boy*. Those became my first words too. He called my parents by their first names. So did I.

My mother took me and Crow to visit my grandparents on a Saturday. She had invited my father, but he said he was too tired for such a long drive, Saturday was his day to take it easy. "Convenient," my mother said. "That's like you."

After eating lunch with my grandparents, my mother dug up saplings from their woods that she meant to transplant, hoping I could climb them and have shade when I was older. The pin oak had been our only tree.

While she planted catalpa and green ash from her parents' woods in our front yard, I played with a plastic dinosaur. Crow played in the dirt, found a sparkling red stone, and dropped it at my mother's feet. My father took it to a work friend who was an amateur rockhound; he looked at it under a special microscope, told him it was a garnet.

"A jewel for my jewel," my father declared when he gave it to my mother, opening his hand slowly, with pride and ceremony.

My mother tried to be happy for him. She didn't tell him that garnets were special but not that special. They were semi-precious—a word that sounded to her like *half price*.

My father invited some buddies from the weedkiller crew to come over and listen to a college football game, the Thundering Herd versus the Golden Flashes. My mother fixed them a platter of deviled ham and crackers, cheese whiz and celery. Our house was small, and the walls were thin, and the men hopped up from the couch, tipped over their drinks, shouted with glee. Mr. Yamato's hands were sore and enflamed; Ned had a rash on his arms; Skidmore said he had no reaction, said the powder never bothered him.

My mother wanted me to nap, so she sent me over to Mrs. Yamato's. She went home so that she could keep an eye on my father. She didn't want him to drink too much. I cried for nearly was an hour, my face angry and red, and Mrs. Yamato could not console me.

"What do you want?" she said. "What's the matter?"

"Crow," I said.

Mrs. Yamato hated crows, but she called my mother and had her bring over Crow in his cage. We all three fell asleep watching variety shows. A lit cigarette slid from Mrs. Yamato's fingers. Crow screamed when the first wisp of smoke curled up from the carpet. I screamed too, but Mrs. Yamato did not stir. She was a heavy sleeper. Crow flung himself at the side of his cage until it fell off the table. Mrs. Yamato woke up. Her curtains were on fire; her carpet was sizzling like bacon. Crow's wing was broken.

"Help," Crow said.

After that, Mrs. Yamato loved Crow. She brought him pickled squid and pink fish cakes when she went to visit her brother in Pittsburgh.

Father splinted Crow's wing. He hopped all over the house while it healed, and I crawled after him.

My mother liked to sing to me and Crow while my father was at work. *All creatures great and small, the Lord God made them all.* My father had told her he did not care for hymns. She tried to get him to explain; finally, he said, "Here's what I believe: there's design, there's atoms, that's it."

My mother said, "How can you not see wonder wherever you look?"

My father said, "That's your Sunday school talking. A bunch of Presbyterian fluff."

When I was big enough to sit in my highchair, my father put Crow's cage on a stool near the table so that we could eat together. My mother saved table scraps for Crow, and my father hunted insects in the yard. While my mother said grace, my father tapped the handle of his fork, did not close his eyes. I folded my hands. Crow hid his head under a wing.

On the Fourth of July, my mother saw blood in my mouth, and then she saw blood in my diaper. She took me to the doctor right away. The medicine was expensive; my parents bought one bottle, then another bottle, and then they were broke. Soon, they were fighting all the time. My mother said we couldn't afford to care for me and also for Crow. She said she wondered if Crow was making me sick—her father had warned her that wild birds carry disease—or maybe it was the factories. She said my father was a fool. He said he was tired of her picking at him. She told him she couldn't believe he would start a family in a place with so much smoke, so much stink. He repeated to her what his buddies said, what the men in our town always said: "That's green smoke, that's the smell of money."

My mother pawned the garnet, her gold necklace, her wedding band. My father drove away, wouldn't say where he was going. Maybe to the beer joint, or maybe the pool hall, or maybe he wanted to be alone and drove in circles. My mother borrowed Mrs. Yamato's car, had her babysit me, drove Crow to Hawks Nest State Park sixty miles to the east, hiked up to the overlook, and let him go.

Mrs. Yamato brought over jars of noodle soup when my mother was too upset to cook. She said she saw a black bird flying over our house every so often. She thought that it might be Crow, but the bird would not land when she called.

I got sicker. I missed Crow. We all did. Supper was the saddest time of day. My father worked overtime. My mother left me with Mrs. Yamato, started bookkeeping at the factory again.

Mrs. Yamato pasted my picture on empty tin cans, took them to every store in town, and in nearby St. Albans and Nitro, and had them placed by cash registers.

One afternoon, while my mother was washing dishes, she looked out the window. There was a trail of black feathers leading from our back door to the shed where my father had once tried to restore a motorcycle. She dried her hands and went out there. She looked for Crow, maybe saw a rag of shadow in the sky, or a speck, or maybe saw nothing at all. The shed was padlocked; my father had the key and wouldn't be home for a few hours. She thought the wood of the shed might be old, rotten, turning soft, but when she tried to pull a loose board, many splinters sunk into her hands. Wondering if there might be a hole in the roof, she leaned a ladder against the shed. She was a little afraid of heights, wasn't sure she wanted to climb up, so she asked Mrs. Yamato, who wasn't scared of anything, now that she had gotten over her fear of crows.

Mrs. Yamato climbed to the roof and peered into the shed. "It looks like a room full of silver," she said.

My mother got an axe, and Mrs. Yamato got a shovel. They struck the door until the wood buckled, and thousands of coins poured out around their feet.

"This is impossible," said my mother.

"I'll get some bags," said Mrs. Yamato.

When my father came home, he and my mother counted enough coins to buy me a bottle of medicine, dropped that amount into a pillowcase, and left Mrs. Yamato to guard the rest. We drove to the drugstore, which had just closed for the night. My father pounded on the door till his knuckles were raw. Finally, the druggist let him in.

My father sat in the backseat and held me, and my mother leaned against him. "I wish Crow would come back," she said.

"Maybe he's been welcomed into a flock of crows. Found a

mate, or a number of his own kind," said my father, and then he leaned over and kissed her forehead.

"Maybe Crow will join a circus," said my mother, patting his hand. "He'll ride in a menagerie car as the train takes him from town to town. While the canvas-men put up the big top, Crow will chat with them. He'll give a lucky feather to a lion cub who has stage fright."

And then my mother poured the glistening medicine into a spoon that she'd brought in her purse. I, too, had an eye for marvelous things, and when she put the spoon in my mouth, I bit the silver hard.

ONLY THE WIND

As far back as she could remember, Rhodie was treated as nothing special: hulky, low to the ground, dough-faced, mud-brown hair. And she never said much of anything.

Cat's got her tongue, her sisters liked to say. They moved their mouths silently, bit their knuckles, made hideous faces to tease her.

Always stooped over, scanning the ground, Rhodie wouldn't look her parents in the eye. If they were too busy or too tired to see her, she didn't want to speak to them. There were summers when she dug bait-worms for her father, springs when she planted iris bulbs with her mother. Most of the time, she was left to do as she pleased.

Rhodie's parents ran the Arbuckle Store and Guest Cottages, which they rented to a few vacationers, and hunters, and fishermen lured there by the Elk River with its *muskies the size of a man's arm*, her father would sometimes boast. Or he might tell the fishermen about *the one I caught the other day, enormous from eating the arms of men*, depending on who the fishermen were, and what he thought he could sell them. When they laughed or snorted in disbelief, Rhodie had seen her father hold up his hand and say, *Gentlemen, I hope to die where I stand if that there fish wasn't sixty-nine inches long.*

Arbuckle, West Virginia, population seven. Rhodie's parents, her two older sisters and brother, and their best customer,

Lionel Smith, a traveling shoe salesman, who rented his cottage by the month. Arbuckle had been the home of oil workers, the makers of barrel staves, men who worked in the gristmill. Now there was no more oil, no more timber, no more grain. Arbuckle was practically a ghost town, cobwebby and creaky, and it smelled like wet grass and bacon grease. Rhodie made a game of counting things that were in the wrong place: a stack of old doors at the end of a street, a porch crammed with rusted machines, the shadows of certain trees that hid from her if she stared at them too long. When she was a child, Rhodie thought Arbuckle was her kind of town. She knew this was not the kind of thing she could tell her family.

Odd duck, her sisters were always calling her.

When Rhodie was ten, she liked walking down the old Coal and Coke Railway, easing through its tangles of multiflora rose; she wished she was brave enough to sneak inside the houses that were boarded up, or vine-covered, or leaning like paper boxes left in the rain.

And she liked spying on Hannah and Gloria, her sisters, who took turns working the cash register in the store. They complained to each other about slow shifts with no customers, about fishermen who were too ugly or too old to flirt with. Rhodie could listen to their every word without either of them noticing she was there. Hannah would roll her eyes, say their father must be an idiot for staying in a godforsaken place like this; Gloria would say she got nervous when the store was empty, what if a robber came in? Hannah was the nasty one; Gloria was high-strung; sometimes, they had vicious arguments and didn't speak to each other for days.

The wind could be fierce in Arbuckle. Rhodie's mother said it was the crying of the pioneer John O'Brien, who had lived inside a sycamore and woken up one morning with his feet frozen to the ground. Rhodie's father said it was the ghost of Wright Childers, whose neighbor beat him to death with a hand-spike following an argument about a rail fence. Another time, when only Rhodie was listening, Lionel said the wind was carrying the lament of the Delaware Indians for five of their families scalped by border-whites and thrown into the river at Bulltown. Lionel was Cherokee. He played poker with Rhodie's father and brother, and paid Rhodie to polish shoes, a nickel a pair. Lionel told Rhodie that when the wind blew, he could sometimes hear children sobbing, mothers praying, fathers calling out as their mouths filled with water.

Rhodie worked for Lionel because she wanted to hear the haint tales and murder tales he collected wherever he traveled. Her mother and her sisters thought his tales were too grue-some and didn't want to hear them; her father said he loved the tales and would pay Lionel to put on a war bonnet and recite them for the entertainment of the cottage guests. Lionel shook his head, said that feathers made him sneeze. Rhodie's mother put her hand on Rhodie's father's arm, told him that he'd been watching too many movies.

Sometimes, when Rhodie sat on the concrete steps of his cottage and shined shoes for him, Lionel asked her, *Would you like to hear a tale?* Rhodie kept looking at the shoes, would whisper the words *yes* and *please*. She learned about coal mine ghosts from Lionel, and an eerie flea-bit stallion surrounded by a blinding light, and a malformed animal with shiny eyes, and headless dogs that crept from the woods on nights with no moon.

And he told her the surveyor William Strange vanished in 1795, and years later his bones and shot pouch and powder horn were discovered under a beech tree at Turkey Run. There was a short poem scratched in the bark above him:

Strange is my name and I'm on strange ground,
and strange it is I can't be found.

And he told her about doors that groaned, branches that scratched the walls of his cottage when the wind was trying to send a message.

Rhodie wanted to share with Hannah and Gloria what Lionel had said, got a few words out before they interrupted her. They giggled, and rolled their eyes, and said that they were too old for silly tales. They said there were no ghosts howling in Arbuckle, that was only the wind. Hannah and Gloria never saw more than one side to a story. They often called her *Toadie*; they liked saying, *Lionel has a little pet, it's named Little Toad.*

Will you all shut your traps, Rhodie's brother would say. *You get uglier when your mouths screech like that.*

Sometimes, Lionel didn't want to tell a story. He would say to Rhodie that he had a headache, then hand her a peppermint stick, nod at her, go inside his cottage, and open the windows so his music drifted out. He played jazz records for Rhodie while she worked with polish, dauber, and lamb's wool, played "Old Joe Clark" and "Muleskinner Blues" while she put shoes back in the sample cases.

Rhodie swiped Lionel's book of poems by Robert Frost when he left it on the dry goods counter. She was twelve. She read it by candlelight in the dark dirt beneath her father's store, where she had made a stable for her toy horses, wired together a corral from pieces of old wood, fashioned a water trough and circus barrels from mud. Trying to mimic Lionel, she read aloud her favorite poem about the snowy evening, the little horse shaking its bells, the miles to go. She experimented with her voice—made it soft, twanged it, pitched it low, made it gravelly—but never got it to sound right.

Then she set the book aside. Her best toy horse was a palomino reared up on its hind legs, speckled with paste she had made from flour and water and flecks of ash. She surrounded the horse with a few lit matches, hoping it would resemble the ghost-horse in Lionel's story. Tired of poems, out of matches, she stockpiled the mud-balls that she would later stash in Hannah and Gloria's hats and gloves and shoes.

Her father whipped Rhodie with a mixing spoon when he found out.

Rhodie wanted to sulk under the pignut tree, saw that her brother had parked his Ford there, was working under the hood. She kicked a tire so that he would look at her. He had taken her fishing a few times; maybe he would be sympathetic.

He frowned when he saw her. He said, "Quit blubbering. If you act baby-fied, Father will smack you like a baby."

Rhodie wished there was a way she could get away from all of them. Sometimes, she would go down to the Elk River, dart from stone to stone to a low saucer-shaped boulder in the middle of the water. There, she would spread herself flat and let the sun pour its warmth over her body; she would cover her eyes with a hand. She would imitate the rush of the water, make whooshing noises with her mouth until she thought she was rushing too, and the boulder beneath her was some strange vessel, heavy and yet miraculously buoyant, and it was spinning her around, making her queasy, light-headed. Maybe even carrying her far away.

One after the other, Rhodie's brother and sisters went to high school in Sutton, the county seat. By the time Rhodie got there, the other kids already knew that she was a little toad. She didn't talk much, even if a teacher called on her. She felt like her mouth was full of marbles, or like her jaws were rusted shut.

So shy, the teacher wrote on Rhodie's report card.

Some kids at high school ignored Rhodie like her family did. Some kids teased her, dared her to speak, to prove that she wasn't an idiot. That stopped the next year when she got bigger, willing to fight back, punch and kick and claw if she had to. She prayed that she would never have to stand before the class and give a book report.

There was an outdoor revival in a torch-lit grove of scarlet oaks on the road to Gassaway. Hannah went every night for a week, invited Rhodie on the last night. Hannah had her eye on the young preacher, said that during every altar call, she went forward, and he would talk to her, lay his hands on her, and she would feel new all over again. Rhodie noticed he was too gangly for his pinstripe suit, had his pale knobby wrists and ankles sticking out. "I'm Spencer Dawson from Ivydale," he said, nodding at his audience. While he preached about the Holy Ghost and the new creation groaning, he grinned earnestly, addressed them as *friends.*

During the dirge-like songs and the clamorous prayers, Rhodie watched the people around her cry and sway, wave their hands, shudder and come loose. The hairs on her arms stood up. Someone shouted, "The spirit is moving here!" Rhodie thought of Arbuckle, the spirits that moved there. Then a little voice popped into her head and told her, *Spirits move around you wherever you go.*

A few women swatted the air as if bees were flying near them, then fell to the ground and rolled over the dead oak leaves; two or three women rested together in a tangled heap. Hannah took off her white sandals, shimmied with her arms stretched overhead. A farmer in bib overalls looked like he was dancing the jitterbug; other men shook tambourines, flatfooted, and hopped over the benches. Rhodie smelled tree sap, and bodies, and the dark circles of sweat that soaked shirts and dresses, the men damp, the women damp, and traces of Ivory soap. So many bodies moving without shame, so many mouths making whatever sounds they pleased: laughter, and whimpers, and a woman howling.

Rhodie did not go forward when there was an altar call. She told herself that someday, when she was older, more confident, she might be ready to cry and sway, come loose, but she had her doubts. A raspy voice behind her called out *you're free, you're free* over and over again. She hoped at least that much was true.

Soon, Hannah married the young preacher. They honeymooned in a guest cottage, kept staying there, had a baby, then another. And then Gloria married a salesman who was Lionel's friend. They too took a cottage, had twins. Rhodie found she was good with babies. She could scrunch her face and make them laugh, or croon a lullaby that soothed tears, or point her finger and scowl to stop childish mischief. On warm spring days, Rhodie would put Hannah's older daughter in a stroller, take her inside the store, through the streets of Arbuckle, down to the river. The tiny girl smiled when Rhodie talked to her, eyed Rhodie thoughtfully when she was silent.

She almost felt like she belonged.

But then blackberry winter came, and the air was cold, and the wind had that sobbing sound again. Rhodie didn't like her sisters and their children as much when she was stuck inside the cottages with them. Hannah was sanctimonious, quick to recite Bible verses, and Gloria saved her good moods for her husband, and the babies smeared mashed carrot on the walls, snatched each other's toys, howled bitterly when Rhodie intervened.

Rhodie's mother told her, "You have the knack with little ones that I never had. My children are dear to me, but if I had it do over again, I'd still be a schoolteacher."

It wasn't like her mother to compliment her. Rhodie decided her mother was warning her: think twice before you give yourself to your sisters' children.

Because the cottages were leaky, had tiny rooms and cheap furniture, Rhodie's father sold them for a song when her sisters and later her brother wanted to buy. (Her brother had been a fireman on an aircraft carrier; he came home with a willowy blonde wife, two stepdaughters, a bulldog.) Fewer fishermen were renting cottages each year, and Lionel had moved back to North Carolina—but Rhodie's father added gas pumps and a repair shop to the store, and Rhodie's brother was the grease monkey, and Rhodie's mother started teaching fourth grade again.

When they were older, Rhodie thought she might give peppermints to her nieces and nephews, tell them some of Lionel's stories. Otherwise, Rhodie tried not to think about the future, what it might hold for her. There was plenty that needed to be done right here. Hannah's older daughter had hair like Rhodie's—limp, flat, the color of old sticks. Rhodie rinsed it with vinegar, combed it with her fingers, made her niece look a little better.

The night before he left, Lionel had given Rhodie a present wrapped with brown paper and baler twine. She opened it a week later, found a can of orange Nehi soda with a letter curved around it. The letter said, *Tell your father and mother I'm going to work for my cousin who's a house carpenter. He looked after me when we were in boarding school. The teachers made him eat soap for speaking Cherokee. I made sure I*

*was quiet as a mouse. When I got home after that, my parents'
cabin was torn down, our farm was seized so Uncle Sam could
run the Blue Ridge Parkway right through it. I stayed with my
family a week or two, and then I had to hit the road. If your
home becomes strange, you might have to leave for a while.*

Rhodie turned eighteen, and her mother and sisters tried to
convince her to stay in Arbuckle. Her father even said he would
give her a cottage, no charge. Rhodie thought about his offer.
But Rhodie didn't like father's pity or the implication that she
might need more help than her sisters. She didn't like being
caught like the rock in the river. And she was tired of feeling like a stranger. She moved to Sutton, went to work at the
Midway Hotel. She was a chambermaid there, making beds
and sweeping floors as she had done in her parents' cottages. Soon, she realized that she hated cleaning as much as she
always had. A few months later, she went to the five-and-dime
and bought a red-haired wig styled in a lofty victory roll, and
she got another job that seemed more exciting: she waitressed
at a restaurant called the Honeybee. With the dramatic wig and
the restaurant's dim lights, with the orange fire lipstick that
Gloria gave her, Rhodie hoped she could transform herself, get
ready for whatever might come next.

One night when she was taking plates of meatloaf and cole-
slaw to a booth, Rhodie thought someone was staring at her,
but that must have been foreknowledge. He turned his head
just as she did, the same angle and speed, so that he first looked
at her the moment she first looked at him. She felt a chill in her
spine and almost dropped her tray. She delivered the meatloaf,
dealt with her customers as fast as she could so that she could
look for him. He asked her to join him at a table.

He said that he was a trombonist; his band was staying at

the Honeybee that night, the next night too. Rhodie told him about Arbuckle; he said his father was a waterman who set out crab pots in the Chesapeake Bay, and he had joined the Navy because he wanted to make a different life for himself. Rhodie said he must like boats. He laughed, and then he asked her if all the girls in Arbuckle were good-looking. She told him that one of her sisters had a nice face, and the other had a pretty singing voice, but had gotten too fat for her girdle.

And then Rhodie said the sentence she had been turning over and over in her mind: "Tomorrow you could ask for a table in my section." It was the boldest thing she'd ever said. It felt like hot coals falling from her lips.

"I'll do that," he said.

When he played with his band, Rhodie watched his lips buzzing against the mouthpiece, the shirtsleeves he rolled up, his brown oxford shoe tapping the floor, the Samoan girl in a grass skirt tattooed on his forearm, her lithe body undulating as he moved the brass slide.

The night after that, Rhodie finished her shift, and she and the trombonist entered the Hokey Pokey Marathon that took place at the Honeybee.

Rhodie had never danced with a man before. She realized that he was a big talker, a big timer, too handsome, too slick. Rhodie could ask him the littlest question and he'd talk her ear off. When she was quiet, he sang bits of song in her ear: *home ain't home* and *Baltimore ain't Baltimore* and *I'd like to ruffle your plumage.* She asked him if he thought they would win the dance. He said ridiculous things: they would be crowned prince and princess, and she would be his true companion, and he would write songs about her. He said he would fix egg-in-the-hole and creamed ham for her breakfast. If she wanted, she could live in his castle, where he had golden plates and crystal goblets, a billiard table and a pretty canopy bed. That was the foolish side of him.

And although she had a feeling there was something sneaky about him, something slippery, Rhodie allowed herself a few modest hopes. That he would write postcards to her, and ask her to send him her snapshot for his wallet. That he would share more of himself. There could be more knowledge, more familiarity, more sparks. For a moment, she imagined him carrying her away on a sailboat, and the spray of saltwater on her face, and a wire basket of crabs with hard blue shells, and the two of them building a fire on a beach.

They were still dancing the next morning, and Rhodie asked him about his service in the Navy. From listening to her brother talk to her father, she had an idea that this was another subject the trombonist would go on and on about.

For once, the trombonist had little to say. The pink faded from his face, and his grip on her loosened. He sounded far away as he said a little about the Battle of the Coral Sea, and the fires he fought when the *Gray Lady*'s fuel lines exploded. Then he was quiet for a long while. Then he closed his eyes and said there were dead men floating in the water, whole bodies, parts of bodies.

He looked like he had seen a ghost. Or like he was a ghost himself.

His stubble had been coarse when his cheek brushed past Rhodie's on the first night of the marathon; it was softer on the second night when the man in the other remaining pair crumpled to the floor and couldn't get up.

Rhodie and the trombonist danced another seven minutes to seal their victory. The manager of the Honeybee handed them a pewter loving cup and a dozen yellow roses, and then a newspaperman asked them to pose for a photograph. That was the last thing Rhodie wanted— her lipstick had worn off, her wig was askew—but the trombonist pulled her close, the sweat of his arm dampened her waist, and then the flashbulb went off, and he kissed her. Kissed her goodbye. He was pining for Baltimore and his girlfriend who was a beautician there, he was ready to settle down, and his band was going to play at a pool hall in Cumberland two nights from now, and he said he would be leaving on the next bus.

Rhodie thought about the dead sailors, thought she could hear anguish in his voice when he talked about his girlfriend, his plans, the pool hall. "I wish you peace," she said.

There was a false side of him that Rhodie had closed her eyes against. She counted the things he had not told her. And counted the things she had not said to him when she found out he was leaving.

Rhodie saw him standing in the doorway of the Honeybee, and then the light changed, and suddenly he was gone, like a snuffed candle, like water down a drain. It was as if he had melted into nothing. She felt a chill in her spine again. For a moment, she wondered if he was ever there.

Rhodie almost didn't miss her family. She recalled the careless words, nobody looking, nobody listening, the long years of ripping deep and sinking their barbs in, and how her sisters had tried since then to mend some of the rips, to whip-stitch the tatters. She could choose which pieces of them she wanted to keep.

And she almost didn't miss the trombonist. She could summon flashes of him until he was standing before her again.

In her own small room on the top floor of the Midway, Rhodie had a narrow bed, a full mirror, an Icy-Hot picnic jug. She had two blue willow teacups and a harmonica, and a framed photo of Gloria and her newest baby, a girl named Genevieve. She had a picture-book of Polynesia that she looked at every day. She had a postcard from Lionel, some pebbles she'd found along the Elk River.

She had learned that the trombonist's eyes were the color of rain clouds. She could bring back the smell of his sweat and his Aqua Velva aftershave, and the ragged tone of his voice when he said, "My ship never wavered. She kept her head up and went down like the Lady she always was."

Rhodie knew the relief of soaking her feet in soapy water, the goodness of her hand rubbing her neck when it was sore. She knew the open hour and the blue note, and the warmth of her own skin, and she knew the sound of her breath.

BAD BLOOD

In the woods behind our houses, we were boys crashing through briars, we were girls pressing ourselves against tree trunks, praying we would fade. We were running from the welfare agents and the school supervisors, the district nurses and the sheriff's deputies who swept through the mountains, looking for us. When our legs burned and our sides ached and we were out of breath, when we couldn't run anymore, we hid, using whatever was at hand. A rotten log to crouch behind. A clump of rhododendron for a screen. The crack in a mossy boulder to squeeze into. We heard them coming for us, heard the dead leaves crackle beneath their heavy feet. We wished that we could run as fast as the deer, or vanish like wisps of smoke. When the agents and the deputies found us, we clung to branches, threw ourselves on the ground, scuffed our feet as they dragged us away.

In the police cars, we were towheaded boys frozen with fear, we were freckled girls thrashing about like trapped animals. We were fifteen years old, or thirteen, or nine. We were accused of truancy, stealing five dollars, begging for food, setting Doubletop Mountain on fire, running around shoeless, seducing an uncle, wearing feed sacks, stealing a chicken, stealing a postage stamp. *I swear that wasn't me.* We were dark-eyed boys with crooked teeth, slender girls with wavy hair. Sometimes, they took our brothers and sisters too, just in case. Sometimes, three or four of us were pushed into the back seats of police cars. People said we were the worst kind; neighbors and store owners and relatives and stepfathers called for us to be moved out, colonized. *Everybody who was drawing welfare was scared they were going to have it done on their children.* People said we were hillbillies, rag tags, dirt eaters, white trash, hollow folk. We lived in shacks with no curtains, or we lived in cabins under the blighted chestnuts, or we lived in weathered houses at the end of rough lanes. Some of us didn't have enough corn bread and salt pork to eat, and some of us had too many brothers and sisters.

Some of us didn't know where the police cars were taking us. Some of us worried that our parents wouldn't be told that we had been taken, would look for us and not find us, would be sick with worry. Some of us had babies of our own, and we never saw them again. We pounded the windows, we kicked the seats, we screamed. *Take me home.* We were accused of degeneracy, pauperism, funny-looking skulls, misshapen faces. We were accused of pregnancy. We were ragamuffins in ripped denim, no underwear. We were unruly children from Brush Mountain, from the hemlock coves below Thunder Knob. We were delinquents from the *dark interior* of the Blue Ridge, where the national park and the tourist road would be, after our families were made to leave.

We were committed to the Virginia State Colony for Epileptics and Feebleminded near Lynchburg. We were locked in brick cottages, in dormitories. At night, we sang all the songs we knew. At night, we told each other that our mothers and fathers would come for us soon, or that we would be sent to live with kind families. We slept in iron beds, under scratchy blankets, on mattresses that smelled like sour milk. When we woke in the morning, we saw ceiling stains, cobwebs, dead flies, red linoleum on the floors, dogs painted on the walls. At night, we gave each other elm leaves and magnolia petals that we had picked that day, that we had smuggled in our shirts. *So your pillow won't stink.*

The doctors at the colony treated us with kitchen chores and laundry chores, barn work and field work. The doctors ordered us to pick strawberries, weave rugs, push brooms tied to twenty-pound weights. The attendants cut our hair with dull scissors, fed us beans and hash. The attendants frisked us twice a day. The doctors diagnosed us as immoral, or low-grade, or furtive, or sullen, or anti-social, or disobedient, or syphilitic, or mentally defective.

When we ran from the colony, the deputies came after us, and caught us, and locked us in solitary, in the blind room, locked us in for thirty days, sixty days. Some of us were kept in the colony for twenty years. Some of us died of fevers, tuberculosis, pneumonia, the flu. Some of us were buried in the colony's unmarked graves.

The doctors gave us shots to numb us from the waist down. *They told me the operation was for an appendix and rupture.* The doctors ordered us to take pills that made us sleepy. *I kicked against it.* They cut into our bellies, cut into our scrotums, clamped off our fallopian tubes, seared our sperm ducts, said they were helping us, said it was for our health. *I thought they were experimenting on us, taking us and butchering us up like hogs.*

We were released on work furloughs, bonded out to cattle farms, boardinghouses, apple orchards, lumberyards, gas pipelines. We were told to please our new employers, to please our new families, to not make a scene. *Be sure you earn an honest living.* Sometimes, we were paid five dollars a month; sometimes we worked but were not paid. We were ashamed. We lied and said we had never been at the colony. Some of us married. Some of us went back to the colony when we had nowhere else to go. Some of us opened our homes to unwanted children, raised them as our own. We didn't talk to newspaper reporters until we were in our seventies. Finally, we could say that our stories ought to be told. We had been children. We had been the rugs they beat to keep their bloodlines rich and clean.

THE ALGEBRA OF LONGING

"I could use a gopher," Uncle Lloyd says, suppertime in June, him on the porch of Jake and Emerson's trailer in Barrackville, shooting the breeze with their father. He won't come in where it's cool, says that he's pretty ripe, he needs a shower. "Don't want to offend the nose of the lady of the house." His tone is a courtly jeer. He tells them that his bride is coming from a sinking island in the Pacific, and the dream house he's building for her isn't close to done.

"Emerson would do great," Jake's father says, waving a fly away. "He's strong as an ox. He'll work his tail off for you."

"He's lazy," Jake blurts out. "Hire me instead." He's surprised that he said it, and so are his father and uncle. They both blink.

"Make that two gophers," Lloyd says. He spits a sunflower hull into the yard. Jake studies his uncle, trying to soak him in: his tie-dyed tank top, his barrel-chested restless body, his bushy moustache and diamond stud earring.

Lloyd tells them she's arriving in August right before the wedding, his foreman herniated a disk, they haven't started sheathing the walls yet.

On the first day, Jake and Emerson find out that Lloyd has plenty of grunt work for them. They carry, fetch, sweep up, ease the labors of Lloyd's construction crewmen who wear

Garth Brooks muscle shirts or fishnet jerseys stretched over their jiggly stomachs, who crew-cut or rat-tail their putty-colored hair.

Emerson ices his sore shoulder that night, sleeps like the battle-fatigued. On his side of the room, Jake squeezes splinters from his palms. He tacks his uncle's discarded blueprints near the map of the moon and the diagram of a protozoan on the wall by his bed. Some of their pay will go to school jeans, polo shirts, Trapper Keepers, and loose-leaf in the fall, some they will spend as they choose. Emerson has an ad for a deer rifle ripped from *Field & Stream*. Their parents are glad Jake and Emerson are making money this summer. Jake wishes his parents had better jobs, jobs they liked. Jake's dad works as a janitor at the hospital, hopes to get his model train store running again. His mom cashiers at Walmart.

As for himself, Jake doesn't know what he wants, doesn't know which of the world's equations he should plug himself into. He is fourteen. There is a strain in him, a yearning for things he doesn't have words for, as if he's starting to upheave, crack apart until he's webbed with lines running in all directions.

Angling the gooseneck lamp, he looks over the plans for the dream house: trophy room, cathedral ceiling, pantry, den. A fireplace of creek stones and a bearskin rug; a kitchen whose shiny gadgets blend, juice, grind, knead, and julienne. Bathrooms with brass dragon faucets; faux bamboo curtains instead of closet doors; a master bedroom festooned with tapestries and tassels. Two smaller bedrooms, in case offspring might be coaxed from the bride's forty-year-old womb.

Jake likes some of Lloyd's phrases. *Things falling into place*, Lloyd says, and *it's all starting to click*. Those words sound good to Jake, and he repeats them to himself, thinks about what they might mean. Jake thinks he might like to have a deposit in the bank, seed money, mimicking his uncle, who saved and saved the profits from his construction company to buy land along Teverbaugh Run Road, and a dream house, and a foreign sweetheart on the installment plan. The road soon passes a Mail Pouch barn and narrows to one lane, dirt for miles and rough as an old corncob, while the run itself is mostly a dribble, a scar of stones and bristly reeds, braided to the road by the concrete slab bridges and drainpipes that it oozes under and through.

Trying to fall asleep, Jake feels the jarring of that road in his spine and eardrums. Lloyd is good at thinking ahead; he's building on the top of a steep hill, high above the run. Flood-proof, he says. He says that his bride lost her house in a monster typhoon and was trapped on her roof with her youngest daughter for three days, waiting for the waters to recede. He wants her to feel safe in her new house. He also worries that she might fall in love with a younger man. His construction crew clicks their tongues or whinnies like stallions when he shows them her snapshot. He wants to live in the middle of nowhere, he says. He wants to keep an eye on his treasure, he says.

When she's not cashiering at Walmart, Jake's mom can usually be found on the left seat cushion of the couch, in a ratty nylon robe, within the wash of soft rock from the radio, windows curtained, the living room dark and sealed as an egg, even in the middle of the day. She never comes into her sons' room. She does tonight. Jake yanks the sheet up to his chin to keep her from seeing him in his underwear. "Lloyd's castle," she says, perching on the edge of his bed, eyeing the blueprints. "That poor woman may wish she was living on the moon instead." She tells Jake she can't sleep, she's going to make his lunch for work, would he like anything special.

Jake yawns, mumbles, gets rid of his mother, but then he can't sleep. Jake imagines his future aunt stuck on a metal roof, surrounded by water and broken trees, waiting for a rescue boat.

Fawn, Lloyd calls him, skittish, ribby, eyes down, watching every step, long skinny limbs. The name sticks, like gum in his hair, dog crap on his shoe. For the summer, each day that Jake works construction, from his uncle, *fawn*. From the men of the crew, *fawn*. And from Emerson, sometimes, *fawn*—and maybe longer, the next year at school, if Emerson repeats it there. Jake works through the lunch break, eats his sandwich on his feet when he's alone, ever since that miserable day when the crew sneered at what his mother had packed for him. For Emerson, three bologna sandwiches. For Jake, one cheese sandwich (because he's picky) and a Bible verse on pretty paper. The crew heehawed, asked if he had a love note from a girl. Emerson didn't betray him. The crew unzips and urinates right in the open, a few steps from ladder or sawhorse, sometimes two of them, hip to hip, laughing, having a contest maybe. When Jake has to go, he slinks off to the stand of dogwoods and decrepit apple trees.

The sun is a blister of fire, the earth around the frame of the house a great amoeba of cracked clay and dozer tread, spotted with cigarette butts and wrappers. Emerson totes shingles, block, brick, drywall. *Hey fawn, sweep this up.* Jake tries to get to the sawdust and stray nails without being told. He digs out poison ivy and burdock, seeds the bare slope between the front of the house and the road, sprays fertilizers, tries to make flowerbeds from railroad ties and manure.

"Think you can plant some trees?" Lloyd says, just the two of them, the crew drilling and sawing on the other side of the house.

"I think so," Jake says.

"Ones that'll grow up slender," Lloyd says. "Like her." His

hands mold a circle in the air. "The email says her waist is that big around." Then he tells Jake more of his landscaping plans. Lloyd lowers his voice, confides in him. He wants Jake to plant cypress and plum trees, douse anthills with poison. The bride, whose hobbies include gardening, will choose her own flowers next spring. "Her heart's desire," Lloyd says, chewing a licorice-flavored toothpick, "assuming I can pay her bills." Her debt to the matchmaking company, K-1 fiancée visa and FBI check, medical exam, vaccines, and plane ticket, all of these familiar to Jake and Emerson, and the crew, who guffaw, slap their thighs, say things like, *Pass me that extension K-1 fiancée thingamajig. I mean cord.*

"Red tape you wouldn't believe," Lloyd tells Jake, man to man.

On the day of the wedding, Jake showers early, avoiding Emerson, who jerks the plastic curtain open on him when he doesn't want to wait, Emerson who takes forever shaving and then gelling his hair. Jake lets his own hair dry any which way, even today. He slips into his backpack the camera and memory card Lloyd asked him to buy at Walmart. Lloyd asked Jake's mother to decorate the little country church on Teverbaugh Run. Last night, she told Jake's father that she didn't have the energy, so Jake's father takes over. Before reaching the church, he parks the car near an overgrown pasture. He widens the gap between two strands of barbwire, saggy and black with rust, one hand lifting, one foot bearing down. Jake eases through, careful not to snag his good pants. A killdeer flashes up from a dip in the ground, scolds them, fakes a broken wing. Jake and his father pick goldenrod and daisies to strew upon the church's windowsills and altar.

Lloyd put the bride in a motel last night. When he brings

her to the church in his Silverado truck with huge off-road tires, Jake and his family are waiting outside. Lloyd darts over, lifts her down from the cab. She wears yards of lilac and brown gauzy stuff wrapped and draped over her small round body, her hair, her face. Only her eyes are uncovered. Jake snaps his first picture.

"Is she Buddhist or Muslim?" Jake's father whispers.

Lloyd has said he'll pay Jake a quarter a picture, a hundred would be good, if Jake can shoot that many. When she applies for permanent resident status, he'll prove that theirs is a relationship of love, not convenience, blessed by a preacher, not a judge.

Lloyd introduces her, mangles the several syllables of her name.

She laughs and says, "Please address me as Lily."

"Have a bridesmaid," Lloyd says. "My brother's wife." Jake's mother raises her hand, flutters her fingers. Jake snaps a picture.

"I carry my daughters with me," Lily says, patting a locket that hangs around her neck. "They are my attendants."

"Let's have a look," Lloyd says.

"That would be bad luck." She hides the locket within the layers of her dress.

"Come on. Just a peek."

Lily's eyes look panicky. She leans away from Lloyd as he reaches for her. Into his open hand, she thrusts a silver flask. "Taste it," she whispers. "Duty free."

Lloyd swigs, hands the flask back to Lily. He wipes his mouth with his hand. Lily tucks the flask into the pocket of his suitcoat.

Jake sees that the wedding guests watch Lily's every move—because she's foreign, or her attire makes her mysterious, or she's so light on her feet, her voice melodious and regal, her black eyes burning everything she peers at. When the preacher tells Lloyd that he may kiss the bride, he flattens his lips against the fabric that covers her forehead. Lily uses the tips of two fingers to graze his chin, travel up his jaw, brush his earlobe.

First day of high school, Jake has sophomore biology, warty Mr. Biji nagging them right away about science fair projects. Jake gets to skip freshman earth science due to his test scores. He finds the room right before the tardy bell rings. The sophomores yammer, carry on, already sorted and paired. Jake thinks they will stare at him as he passes to the empty desk at the back of the room. But no one does. Mr. Biji takes attendance. His swept-back hair looks like a Treasure Troll's. He says, "Did I miss anyone?" Jake raises his hand. But Mr. Biji is already distributing project guidelines. "Do you want a pair project, or an individual? Brainstorm with your seatmate." He sets the guidelines on Jake's desk, then yanks them away.

"Who are you?" he says. Jake tells him his name. At the lectern, Mr. Biji consults his roster, finds a strip of paper stapled to the back, glares at Jake. "So now I have to keep track of a freshman roster. Great. This isn't a cake class. I don't wipe noses. Do you understand?"

Jake says, "Yes." His voice is a croak.

"Anyone still looking for a partner?" Mr. Biji asks the sophomores, but they drown him out, their jokes, gossip, pastimes, and preoccupations a sea that pounds Jake's ears, lifts him, lowers him. He bobs along, microscopic as plankton.

After school, while Emerson goes to football practice, Jake helps Lloyd put the finishing touches on his dream house. Lily has stationed herself at the kitchen table with thank-you cards, instruction booklets for her appliances, a stack of cookbooks. She wears knee-length shorts and a blouse printed with seahorses. Jake rinses his brush at the sink, gets it clean, lets the water run, pretends he is still rinsing the brush. He's evading Lloyd, who wants Jake to put on his stinky old coveralls, unwashed and too big for Jake, and join him in the attic to put down insulation in the narrow spaces that only Jake can fit into.

"I want to cook something for you," Lily says. Her uncovered face seems dull and old. She hides her crooked teeth behind her hand when she talks. "Because you worked so hard on the grounds, and the young trees. And I want to cook a fancy supper for my husband." She motions for Jake to come closer, continues in the scarcest whisper. "He won't take me to the store. But I want to do things. I want you to buy ingredients. Vegetables. Some good beef."

Jake says, "You don't have to. You should settle in first." She may or may not know that Lloyd is threatening to send her back to the island and file for an annulment. He says that Lily passed off photos of her eldest daughter as photos of herself, claimed she was forty instead of fifty-one, and much thinner, and got him drunk on his wedding night. When he finishes the house, he'll deal with Lily. Until then, he brings home take-out fried chicken in the evenings. He sleeps on the couch, but then wakes up to find her standing near him in a negligee. All this mess causes Jake's father to go out night after night to have long talks with Lloyd at a bar. And animates his mother, who rehashes the details to anyone who doesn't hang up on the phone or back out of the room. And makes Jake say, "If I have to hear about his sex life one more time, I'll puke."

Lily insists that Jake sit at the table and look through her cookbooks. She brings him a bowl of sweet sticky rice, gets him to talk about his first day of school.

"I was a laboratory technician in my country," Lily says. "Perhaps I can help you with the fair." She says that she lived a mile from the ocean, and she lost her first house in a hundred-year flood, and built a new house on stilts, and then lost the new house in a worse flood a year later that carried away her water tank, flattened her garden wall, damaged her grandparents' graves, uprooted her yellow flame and rosewood trees. All over her island, there were mudslides, and coconut trees blown down, and cell phone towers snapped like twigs, and roads and yam farms and taro pits buried by debris. Lily says that when the storm was over, the islanders set to work clearing the rubble with chainsaws and trash fires, and there were days of smoke.

Jake forgets that Lloyd suspects the worst of Lily, that his dad calls her a con artist. He hears laughter, footsteps, Lloyd bringing the hot tub installation man into the kitchen for a beer.

He says to Jake, "Am I paying you for snack breaks?"

Jake shuts the barbecue cookbook.

Lily kisses Lloyd's hand. "He's explaining the words I don't know," she says. "So that I can make breakfast for your bed."

Lloyd hands a frosted mug to the installation man. "All right. She's your boss too," he says to Jake. He raises his fist to slug Jake in the arm, reconsiders, pats him instead.

Jake zooms out of fourth period history, bypasses his locker, hurries through the crush of bodies in the stairwell, but it doesn't matter. He never gets to the cafeteria soon enough, there aren't enough tables, he must chance sitting with a neutral acquaintance, a variable in denim, a wildcard stranger. Experiments of luck. Jake dodges Emerson and his friends; if he thinks they see him, he stares at his tray of pale vegetables and meat nuggets. When he asks some ex-allies from middle school if he can sit with them, his voice cracks. Another time, he joins a table of girls without asking. They ignore him until their pimpled ringleader passes him a note folded into triangles that says, "ZAP! I just shot you with my drop-dead gun."

On a night his father gets home from work early, Jake tells him that he needs more eggs for his science fair project. His father says, "Can it wait? I'm bone-tired." His mother calls out, "Give me the keys. You must think it's safe for me to drive after dark." His father relents. At the community bulletin board in the entryway of Foodland, Jake pins a hand-lettered sign advertising Lily's services as a seamstress of Halloween costumes. She wants to earn her own money. Lloyd takes her shopping now, but he stalks along behind her, tracks her every move.

Jake helps Lily a few times a week. She asks him to proofread her writings, shows him her design for a high-yield vegetable garden she will plant in the spring, asks him to interpret some of the words in her catalog of medicinal herbs. She seeks his counsel on the intricacies of American social customs. She calls it "tutoring." He would call it *plotting*. Striding through her dream house, surfing the TV's thirty-seven channels, storing up all that she observes and hears for future use, she is a whirl of plastic beads, a whiff of sandalwood and tamarind paste.

Jake thinks about his biology class, his desk that nobody wants, the feeling that he's plankton, tossed by the sea. Now he and Lily sit together at her table, and maybe she feels lost, but she's adapting fast, she seems determined, unflappable. He tries to figure her out. She speaks three languages. She has commandeered the trophy room because of its abundant light, set up her sewing machine and statue of Buddha near the sliding glass doors. She cajoled Lloyd to take down his deer heads, warning him of karma. Two buckets, one for the walnuts she has gathered, the other for hickories, stand against the wall of what is now her sewing room. When the buckets are full, she says she will sell the nuts. She irons shirts for the preacher at the country church, launders tablecloths for Mr. Yau (who owns a Chinese restaurant in Fairmont), and sells to Jake's father an herbal tea that she blends herself, which he swears is a sleeping aid and a boon to his kidneys. Lily also convinced Lloyd to buy her a dozen hens. She says that Jake can observe them for his science project if his egg project doesn't work; in return, she asks him to teach her the vocabulary words for Honors English that he's quizzed on weekly.

The trouble is, Jake isn't getting very far with the eggs. The best he can do right now is hard-boil an egg, put some shredded newspaper inside a glass bottle and set the paper on fire, then place the egg on the mouth of the bottle. The changing air pressure forces the egg to slide into the bottle with a loud pop, to fit inside a space where it does not belong. But Jake doesn't see how this proves much of anything.

Jake tries to persuade his mom to attend Lily's dinner party. His mom frowns at the beige wool scarf she's knitting, unravels a few stitches. She sits on the couch, as usual, though she's turned on the lamp with circus elephants painted on its shade. Jake considers its puddle of light a hopeful sign.

"Your uncle doesn't like me," she says. "I don't have an outfit."

Jake holds up her fleece-lined moccasins. "Wear what you have on," he says.

She knits another row. "And Lily is making her sewing students act like waitresses. Lah-dee-dah." Her needles clack like fencing sabers.

Jake says. "Please? Just this once?" He wants to say, *just this once, do something for me.*

"Parties give me headaches. Headaches make me cry." His mom reaches for a tangled skein of aquamarine yarn, plunges her fingers into the snarls.

"So does sitting in this room all day," he says.

"Your aunt and uncle are always fussing. They make me tense," she says. "Did you comb your hair?" She touches his cheek. "Sweetie, it's like this. I feel everything too much. You don't know how hard that is."

"Lily wants to get to know you better," Jake says.

His mom squints at him. "You're so interested in her. Your super aunt. Your magnificent island auntie."

"Can't you give them a chance?" Jake says.

"He's a bully. She uses people. Why not spend the evening with me? We could watch TV. Play cards."

"It's really important," Jake says. He doesn't say, *to her*. Doesn't say that he was helping Lily cook last night. He hides his hands behind his back so his mother won't see his fingers still yellowed from the turmeric he sprinkled on ten pounds of prawns that he de-veined himself, still smarting from the birds-eye chilies he chopped into slivers.

Jake's father is there, and Lily's sewing students, Sabrina and Jill, dressed in white tops and black pants like waitstaff in a classy restaurant. They shoo Jake from the kitchen when he offers to help; they carry the steaming platters of basmati rice and prawn curry to the table, then chat with Emerson, sit on either side of him.

Lloyd plunks an antacid tablet into his glass of water. "My wife's already burnt away half my stomach," he says. "The spicier she makes it, the more I eat too much."

"Maybe I'll just eat rice," Jake's father says.

After diluting his tea with coconut milk, Emerson downs it in two gulps. Jill pours more tea into his cup. "I think it's cool that you're learning about another culture," Emerson says to Jill. She invites him to go to Spanish Club with her.

Lily wears a peach-colored dress with sleeves like wings. She serves Lloyd his own individualized plate. She whispers in his ear. "Dig in, everybody," Lloyd bellows.

Glancing at green-eyed Sabrina, Jakes tries to see how much rice and curry she spoons onto her plate, how she reacts when she takes her first bite.

Lloyd's face reddens; droplets fall from his eyes, and hairline, and nose. Lily urges him to eat a sago pearl-ball soaked in syrup, to take some of the fire away.

"Lloyd, can I come over when deer season opens?" Emerson says.

"Sure thing," Lloyd says.

But then Lily lowers her fork, moves her hand beneath the table; maybe she gives his knee a hard squeeze, or maybe her touch is feather-soft. "I mean," says Lloyd. "Nature is tricky, right? I think we should give our local deer the year off. Try living harmoniously?"

Lily gives Lloyd a pleased look, holds her napkin to her mouth, which must mean she's smiling at him.

Jake tries not to formulate the algebra of longing, to fool himself into thinking that if Lloyd's attraction to Lily is magnified by the food she cooks for him, then Jill and Sabrina, assuming they enjoy the prawn curry, will in some way acknowledge or appreciate him as Lily's helper. Jake rode his bike to the Chinese restaurant to pick up ingredients from Mr. Yau, minced the green ginger, soaked the tiny, salted fish in cold water. He thinks that Lily will thank him later. During the meal, keeping Lloyd fed and watered, fired up and cooled off and fired up again, takes most of her attention.

Emerson volunteers to help the girls wash the dishes. "Don't you dare splash me," Jill says.

"I'll help too," Jake says.

No one replies.

He follows them into the kitchen anyway. Jill and Emerson run water into the sink. Sabrina scrapes plates into the trash can. Her shirt is velvety, with a rhinestone at the base of her neck and a cut-away part, exposing a teardrop of her back.

Jake asks her what her favorite class is, what music she listens to. He looks for something to throw away—onion peels, crumpled foil—but Lily's kitchen is too tidy.

Then Sabrina actually answers him. Sort of. She says, "You're going about it the wrong way. You need different approaches. Try to sound confident. Friendly. Not so desperate."

Jake says, "Thanks."

Sabrina takes a dishtowel from a drawer, joins the assembly line of Jill washing and Emerson rinsing. Jake maintains his position near the garbage can, does not leave. In a few minutes, when they realize that they don't know the shelves where Lily keeps her dishes, or the drawers where she puts her utensils, Jake becomes useful to them.

The forecast calls for snow in mid-November. Thanks to Lily's negotiations with Mr. Yau, Jake has made about a hundred dollars so far, from scavenging Lloyd's woods for old deer antlers. Mr. Yau grinds up the antlers and packs the powder in plastic canisters that he ships to China. According to Lily, deer antler is a yang herb that enhances life force and longevity, fortifies the back, knees, and midsection. For his science fair project, Jake is testing the effects of powdered deer antler on mice. The five mice of his experimental group already look bigger and longer, their coats glossy and sleek.

In geometry class, Jake guesses the correct number of agate marbles in a jar, wins a chocolate parabola that weighs fourteen ounces. He wants to give it to his mother. She's making meat loaf when he gets home. He watches her roll the glob of hamburger in bread crumbs and form it into a log, smash the log and try a new shape, flatten that too and sculpt a perfect brick.

"I have something for you," Jake says. "You don't have to eat it." He offers her the cellophane-wrapped chocolate.

Her face lights up, and then she cries. "Sweetie, I'm so touched." She goes to the sink to scrub her hands. "But I'm dieting. I'll feel better about myself if I drop a few pounds. Give it to your father. He loves candy."

After school the next day, Jake takes the chocolate to Teverbaugh Run. "Kick your shoes off. The floor's just been mopped," says Lloyd, who's sitting at the table.

"By your uncle," says Lily, rubbing his shoulder, hot glue gun in her other hand.

"I like it done a particular way, all right?" says Lloyd. He moves his hands in an arc. Lily attaches a magnet to a felt turkey.

"I brought you this," says Jake, pulling the chocolate from his backpack.

"A candy horseshoe?" says Lloyd.

"For our anniversary?" says Lily. "Jake, your mother told you. Didn't she? Lloyd and I are celebrating three months of our new life." She holds up her hand, makes a little pushing motion. "We have special plans for this evening."

Jake forgets to hand over the chocolate. He slides the glass door open, just wide enough for him to slip through sideways. The cypress and plum trees he planted are skinny as pencils. He walks into the woods behind the dream house, crunches through dead leaves, a few tomato-red or dandelion-yellow, most of them nondescript brown.

He traipses past black cherry and locust trees, past heaved-up boulders dotted with rosettes of lichen. Teverbaugh Run is still high from the October rains, its hopping stones submerged—too full for him to cross, a line that closes him in.

In five minutes—maybe longer, maybe the flow of time is different in woods like these—he feels the woods surrounding him, encircling him. The patchy clouds have multiplied, clumps of them swelling, graying the sky. The sun loses its brightness, blinks, wavers, like an eye trying to flush out a speck of sand.

Jake zips his jacket, throws the chocolate over his shoulder. He hasn't found any antlers for two weeks. Still, the changeable light may fool his eyes. When he glimpses a forked stick up ahead, he tells himself that it is more than just a forked stick, that it glows and hums, could be an arrow pointing to another set of answers, a way forward.

In the Hollow

Sam and Leah moved from one disappointing house to another the first few years they lived together. Their jobs had them on the road much of the time—Leah as a home health aide, Sam driving as far as Charleston to work for her uncle, a countertop installer. They kept hoping they could find a place in Guyandotte County that was cheap, quiet, with enough natural light for her to paint still lifes, and for him to glue, knot, and wire together his objects.

"Mixed media sculptures," Leah had called them, early on in their relationship. It was the first time Sam was brave enough to show her what he had been working on, cow skulls tied together with Christmas lights and mounted on found wood, stored under a blanket in the bed of his pickup. When he peeled the blanket even further back, there were a few dozen empty cans of Treet lunch loaf that Sam had shot with his brother's rifle, and then a bunch of can keys strung together like a necklace.

Leah said that Sam's assemblage in the truck-bed was saying something important, that she liked how he was fighting the industrialization of meat, the torture of animals.

Sam didn't want to tell her that his art wasn't that complicated. "So now you've seen my junk jumbles," he said sheepishly, and he ran his fingers through his curly hair.

"Don't bash your vision," she said, and put her hand on his shoulder, as if she was steadying him.

*

There was an old company house in Burnerville that smelled like coal dust and rotting wood and had humpback crickets swarming the cabinets. And then there was a tiny garage apartment in Clevenger that Leah's uncle owned, crowded with junky furniture, the oven door almost bumping the foot of the bed. And then a fixer-upper on Sam's mother's place near Mullins Tipple, surrounded by overgrown lilacs and yuccas and wisterias that set off Leah's allergies.

After that, a secluded two-story with asphalt siding, a well that went dry in the summer drought, house sparrows that chittered in the attic, and scrub pines grown through the ruined back porch. Sam wanted to nail up sheet metal to close the holes in the attic, get the sparrows to quit nesting there. Leah didn't want him to bother them. Sam said that they had to draw the line somewhere.

"I know you could care more if you tried," she said.

"Don't they destroy the eggs of other birds?" he said. "They're invaders. An alien species. Let's run them off."

"Should we run off humans too? We're the worst enemies of birds."

Leah took out her field guide on eastern birds, learned all that she could about house sparrows, and put trays of millet and cracked corn on the ground. She repaired the folding attic stairs so that she could go up and watch them. Before dropping out of college, she had wanted to become a field biologist, maybe a wildlife illustrator. Leah was a house sparrow enthusiast for a while that summer; she studied them, painted them, talked about them. Sam picked up her field guide, made a tiered birdbath from trashcan lids because there was no rain. He also read about house sparrow aggression, found a dead bluebird in the driveway, did some more research. If Leah changed her mind, he thought he would offer to help her make ground traps, capture the sparrows, cut their flight feathers.

The landlord raised their rent—and the house sparrows were still jabbering in the attic—when Sam and Leah decided to look for another place. Sam found them a drafty bungalow with rust-brown carpets, too close to Route 3, coal trucks rattling by all night. In the winter, Leah tried painting with mittens on, gave up, found chores to do, or watched *Wheel of Fortune*, or napped. She didn't complain, and that worried Sam. Usually, she would say, *we can do better.*

When the heating bill for the bungalow was painfully high, Sam said, "I think we should move."

Leah was in the living room, scrubbing at a stain in the carpet. She said that she couldn't stand another dump.

"I'll keep looking," Sam said.

Sam and Leah had different ways of finding places to live. Sam checked bulletin boards at convenience stores, scanned newspapers and circulars, watched for signs while he drove, kept the phone numbers of everyone he knew so that he could call around. He plodded, tinkered, accrued.

Leah was slapdash. She waited on chance conversations with strangers, or her uncle's schemes, or surprise house-sitting invitations. Sometimes, she had a tug of intuition while driving that compelled her to make a sharp turn, venture up a steep dirt road, ford a creek—and sure enough, come to a rental sign.

Another week of bitter cold had gone by—a week when Leah taped more plastic sheeting on the windows, and Sam unfroze the pipes with his arc welder—and then Leah came to him with a possibility while he was sorting through his collection of scrap metal. She had seen a place for rent on her way back from checking on an elderly couple in Burnerville, and she had a good feeling about it.

"The trouble is, I had gotten a little lost, and now I'm not sure which road I was on," she added.

Sam said that he wished she would be more methodical.

"You're one to talk," Leah said, smiling. "You pretend to go house-hunting, but really you're junk-hunting."

Sam knew she was right. When he checked the papers and the roads, he was always looking for the discards and freebies that sidetracked him.

"You could try writing a note to yourself," he said.

"My way gets results," she said, almost an accusation.

Reproach could run both ways. Sam wanted to say something sharp, to think of words that would push back, but he just stared at Leah, her paint-spattered flannel shirt, her copper-penny eyes, her uneven ponytail, her breaths puffing out as clouds in the cold room that had frost flowers on the windows every morning.

They went out looking for the house Leah had chanced upon while she was lost. Sam used the GPS on his phone to guide him to the general area and a handwritten list of side roads, while Leah drove her Subaru in circles. She had said she would go *the crow way* And then they both pulled into the driveway of the house almost at the same time, Leah arriving about a minute sooner. It was a farmhouse in the hollow off of Packville Road.

Later that day, the owner took them inside, pointed out the beadboard walls and stone fireplace and the creek in the ravine out back. Leah said that she loved it. She and Sam moved in, got rid of the cobwebs and dead wasps, scoured and mopped, unpacked and organized. After the farmhouse felt like a home, they sat at the top of the ravine and listened to the creek gurgling over its stony bed.

The love they had then was heated and ravenous, wood smoke and patchwork quilts, blackberry wine and cinnamon candles, red trillium and sweet everlasting, tonic and salve.

Leah made the smaller bedroom her painting studio. Sam said that he would raise seedlings, sell vegetables and herbs. He was thinking about objects he could make from turban gourds and toothpicks, pipe cleaners and milkweed pods.

"It'll be different now," Leah said the first week they lived there.

"I hope so," Sam said.

The sides of the ravine were shale and clay, too slippery to get down. For a closer look at the creek, Leah walked down the road, unfolded a camp chair, and sat under the slab bridge that crossed it. She was gone for hours. When Sam asked what she was working on, she showed him her sketches: ripples flowing around a series of mossy stones, tiny flies hatching in dense clouds, the refracted sunlight.

She kept asking him to join her, and eventually Sam did go with her to the creek. He rolled up his jeans and waded with her to the edge of a swimming hole not far from the bridge, and they took their clothes off and went in. Sam thought the water smelled funny, maybe a little like rotten eggs, maybe like licorice, but he said nothing. He didn't want to spoil her enthusiasm.

He thought about how withdrawn Leah had been last winter, when they lived in the chilly bungalow. She was mopey, closed off. Sam had puttered along like always, he did chores, halfheartedly tried to recycle some materials he knew he would never use. He made scrap metal reindeer, sold a few of them; he stayed busy because he thought that an awful feeling might seize him if he stopped, some dread or defeat.

Maybe the cold weather had been depressing them, maybe geography. Sam and Leah had long commutes, and they drove through a lot of Guyandotte County. If they wanted fresh vegetables and meat, they had to drive an hour to the nearest super center, then an hour back. Sometimes, in hushed voices, they told each other what they had seen. Too many sad little towns and boarded-up grocery stores, and billboards that read "Coal keeps the lights on" and "Coal powers the nation," too many ruins left by deep mines, rusted tipples and battered conveyors and coke ovens, and memorials for miners, black helmets and red crosses, white tulips and dark granite etched with the shapes of the dead, and the savage upheaval of mountaintop mines, giant dozers and draglines gouging the earth, and valley fills and blasted ridges, creeks stained with yellow boy, and the mountains laid bare.

Now, spring was coming, and they had settled into the farmhouse in the holler, between unbroken ridges that folded around them like hands. Leah was inspired, full of energy, but Sam was not. When she wasn't working, Leah was drawing the creek. She was unfurling, Sam thought. Let her draw all day, what was the harm? Let them live like hermits in parallel worlds. Sam was happy for her, or mostly happy, a little jealous. He wanted the attention she gave the creek, or some of it. He varnished some gourds, cut pictures from *Life* magazines, made some popsicle stick people with googly eyes and panting yarn tongues because Leah always laughed at those. That was as far as he got with his projects. He was stuck, or he didn't have enough motivation. He had seedlings to thin, and raised beds to build, and old leaves to collect for the compost pile.

Sam walked outside and saw dogwood and service-berry trees blooming. Frog eggs glistened in patches of muck where the ground was swampy.

A coal truck drove up the road, and he wondered if there was a mine portal somewhere in the holler. He had thought there weren't any mines nearby.

One day when Sam was planting lettuce, Leah came to him, ready to talk. Her face was flushed. Her hair was muddy, her jeans too.

"You should see what's living in the creek," she said.

"Tell me," he said.

"Caddis-fly larvae that make their own shelters from silk and grit."

"I'll check it out after I finish up."

"And whirligig beetles that have two pairs of eyes," she said. "One for seeing above the surface and the other for seeing underwater." The cuffs of her flannel shirt were wet, as if she had dipped her hands in the creek. "I'm going back."

"Don't stay away too long," Sam said. He didn't think she heard him.

When he went inside, he put on his coat. There was ice breath in the farmhouse, and a dead daddy longlegs in the sink, and in the hearth, a mound of cool gray ash.

On a warmer day a few weeks later, Sam and Leah were wading the creek upstream. Leah had sold four small watercolors to a coffee shop in Charleston, all views of the creek from the slab bridge, and Sam had suggested that they look for more scenes for her to paint.

"I can't find a new subject just by willpower," Leah said. "Or whatever it is you think I can switch on."

"I'd still like to get to the top of the ridge," Sam said.

In old running shoes and track pants pushed up to the knees and faded tee-shirts, they clambered along. Sometimes they hopped from stone to stone, and sometimes they waded, kicking up water.

They followed the creek's twists and meanders, and passed by a few houses and trailers. They invented names for the feeder branches and forks. In a low spot where the hemlocks and laurels bowered over them, Leah told Sam to hunker down. She pointed out tiny columns of mud rising from the bottom. "Crawfish chimneys," she said.

When he stood up from the water, Sam saw that his shirt-hem was tinged yellow. "What's this?" he said.

"Sweat stains," Leah said.

They kept wading until they came to a chain-link fence that ran across the creek and into the woods on either side. The fence was hung with No Trespassing signs, another sign that bore the name of the company who now had a claim on the land upstream.

"That's weird," Leah said.

"Maybe to keep four wheelers out," Sam said.

Leah had brought sketching supplies in a snap bag; she took out paper and jotted the company's name and phone number.

And then about a week after they waded the creek, Leah dashed into the farmhouse. Sam was making frames for her pictures, honeysuckle braided with grapevines. "Something's wrong with the creek," Leah said. "The fish are swimming funny, like they're drunk." And then she was gone, running down the road to the slab bridge.

When Sam got there, Leah was standing in knee-deep water, surrounded by dead fish, belly-up, lifeless little ovals. She lowered her cupped hands into the water, lifted the fish, let them spill back into the creek, lifted more fish out. She was repeating their names: *minnow, muskie, shiner, darter.*

Sam thought the dead fish all looked the same.

The creek widened and got shallower a few feet from where Leah stood, and Sam could see clots of white slime coating the creek-bottom, maybe algae, or trash, or maybe something like paint. "Get out of there," he said.

Leah shuddered but stayed where she was.

A pickup crossed the bridge, and jerked to a stop, and pulled off to the side. An old woman rolled down her window and poked her head out. "Don't you people know that's sick water," she said. "Ever since they put a cleaning plant at the head of the hollow. Ever since they dug a bunch of slurry ponds that spill over when it rains."

Leah stopped going to the creek. When she and Sam talked about moving now, Leah didn't say that she was tired of dumps. She said, "I love it here and now I hate it too." She said that she felt poisoned, not just her body but something deeper, and when Sam said he wanted to help, she said she didn't think he could. "I know the creek is not a thing you care about," she said. She had smudges under her eyes.

Sam thought that Leah had stopped drawing and stopped eating too—when he offered to cook something, she said she had a headache, she had no appetite. But then he snooped in her studio while she was at her cousin's baby shower. Her desk was littered with rice cake crumbs and empty mustard packets. The top sheet of her sketchpad was blank; he turned to the next sheet, almost didn't see the tiny female humanoids penciled in the bottom left corner. One encased within a tube of pebbles, and one armored with quills and bristles, and one who had beetle-eyes.

After Leah quit going to the creek, Sam tried to take up where she left off. He missed how exuberant she had been when she was drawing the creek; maybe he could get her connected with it again, or maybe knowing the creek would be a way for him to know whoever she was becoming. Early each morning, before he drove to work for her uncle, he went to her spot under the slab bridge, added notes to a journal he was keeping, sometimes a rough sketch. He thought he might build a diorama of the creek scene; he would enjoy the repetitive work of gluing and detailing the tiny set-pieces. Most of the notes he recorded in the journal were mundane; there might be discarded beer cans disrupting the sameness of the creek, occasionally a faint odor, but that was it.

Sam also visited the neighbor who had told them about the cleaning plant at the top of the holler. Her name was Flutie Johnson, and she was in her housecoat and work boots, weed-eating the steep part of her front yard, when Sam stopped by. She had covered her pickup with blue tarps. She said that there was a silo full of coal dust up the road; on a windy day the dust came down in clouds and got all over her marigolds and yard gnomes. The company that owned the ridge had put renewal permits in last week's *Coal River News*. When Sam didn't say anything, Flutie said, "That means they're ready to expand the sludge ponds." She went inside, brought out the newspaper and showed Sam the permits, and gave him a glass of dandelion tea. She said she had made it from store-bought water. Sam winced when he saw that his glass had bits of vegetation floating in it.

I need to tell Leah this, Sam thought. *Get through to her somehow.* Maybe she would decide to move; maybe she would want to fight for the creek; maybe she would snap out of the slump she was in.

When he went into her studio, it sounded like Leah was scribbling aimlessly. He heard the rapid scratching of her pencil as she slid it around and around. She said, "Hey," but didn't look at him; she was leaning over the pad, her face almost touching the paper, as if whatever haphazard thing she was creating required her full concentration.

He said, "Do you want to stay here?"

She kept her eyes down, took out a kneading eraser, dabbed the paper, then sharpened her pencil against a sanding stone. "Maybe. I think so," she said. "But I've got a bad headache." She turned her chair toward Sam, sat there facing him. "I can't paint. Is my hand shaky?"

She held out her right hand; it reminded Sam of some neglected plant, drooping and stained, desperate for sunlight.

"We could move out of state," he said.

"We have people here," she said.

"I don't know what you want," he said.

"Are you ever going to ask what I'm working on?" she said.

At first glance, a quick flip through Leah's pad, Sam felt anxious. It looked like a stranger's work. Pages of chicken tracks and zigzags and curlicues. He saw random markings, irregular shapes, chaotic slashes. Leah was watching him, tapping her pencil against the table, and Sam tried to keep his expression neutral.

When he gazed carefully, when he gave a long look to one page of Leah's swirls and slashes, and then to another, he saw gusts of wind clearing rubble from the earth, and then diagonals of rain that might wash it clean, put out the burning, and then potent loops and eddies coming off the page.

THE LABOR OF HER HANDS

Three bad crop years, too much drought, too much soil-wash, smuts and Hessian flies on the small grain, and armies of worms nibbling holes in the tobacco leaves. Olivia's father said he could hear the grinding together of all those tiny worm-mouths, it was the sound of a low constant wind, a dry rattling cough, in his ears when Hubbard dressed him at sun-up, still in his ears that night when he dreamed. He said the turkeys he had deployed were a failure. He said all available hands must make a thorough inspection of the tobacco plants, find and destroy the worms, leave none alive—elderly, invalid, and all the children on the plantation, white and black, his included. Olivia's mother asked if meant to omit John Penny. That was just the thing to rile Olivia's father. John Penny was a Tutelo boy he'd won in a card game, along with a cider press and a hogshead of rum. You know what I mean, Olivia's father said.

The one crop that thrived was the lima beans, dense leafy bushes weighted down with pods. In fields sun-scalded, shimmering from the heat, Olivia worked the tobacco, the lima beans. In the kitchen, her mother told Indian Nan to teach her how to put up the limas, then went to the springhouse to supervise the butter-churning. Nan showed Olivia the kegs, the mounds of salt, the stone-weights. Olivia asked if she was a relation of John Penny's, were they from the same tribe.

Olivia thought Nan wasn't going to reply, but eventually

she said no, said her people had sometimes disputed the Tutelo.

Olivia said, "But I see him with you all the time, as if you were his kin perhaps."

Another long silence, and then Nan said that they shared a hut in the quarters, and in addition to that, they both knew the sadness of losing family.

Olivia said, "Did you have babies?"

Nan said, "Let me see your hands." She peered at Olivia's grimy nails, the dirty green smudges on her palms, the fine scratches. She poured water into a basin, mixed in a sour-smelling liquid from a dark bottle. "Soak your hands in this," said Nan. "It's vinegar of the four thieves. It'll smart but you'll have lady hands again." Nan clamped her long rough hands around Olivia's hands and plunged them in.

Daughter with
a Star on Her Brow

July

Kasia murmurs to herself, zigzags from one side of the road to the other. She gives the neighbors a good look at her gangly frame, frazzle hair, fox eye. She brings water from the pump at the end of the road, the bucket filled only partway, all the better for the wasting of the morning. For avoiding that two-room shanty, the flies, the biscuit crumbs, dribbles of syrup, her mother in bed again with a wrung-out face and blanched skin and pumpkin belly.

Give Kasia sun-scorch instead, and pine branches, and the pigweed and nightshade vines choking the pump, and the see-sawing of her arms as she works the pump handle, and the gurgle of water. These she loves, and the spooked shadows of the neighbor-girls fleeing. She knows they ridicule her. They cross to the other side of the road, yammering as if she can't listen to both them and her own muttering.

Water for boiling the cabbage, water for scrubbing the floors, water for the baths of brothers and sisters, and for father. Idled these last three days, and still pinches of coal dust sprinkle off him wherever he goes, especially upon the surfaces Kasia has just wiped. He sleeps late, wakes to sit vigil at her mother's bed. He wipes her mother's forehead, fans her if she sighs, helps her sit up for broth and tea. He goes outside after breakfast to play with Kasia's brothers and sisters, and again after supper, insisting that in his absence Kasia sit with her mother and fuss over her. Something she never does when he's at work in the mine. If Kasia balks, his neck-vein pulses, his eyes burn, he threatens. She gives in. But as soon as he closes the door, Kasia drags his chair to the foot of her mother's bed, away from her mother's rancid breath, condemning eyes. She covers her mother's feet, two dead fish, too awful to look at. She listens to her father and brothers and sisters as they play ball, or charades, or lion sleeping in the grass, are you brave enough to tiptoe past.

Kasia wishes that he could be like this always, teasing and tickling and chasing her brothers and sisters. That her mother would get better, cook and clean again. That she could go traipsing in the woods, search for campion and starflowers to press between the pages of her mother's Bible. She keeps her favorite pinecones in an old crate. Sometimes, she discovers a cross-shaped fragment of branch, and these she also saves. When she was little, she tried to take the beaded Star of Bethlehem from the nativity creche at church, but it was glued to the magenta foil backdrop, and then her mother pinched her arm and said, "You may look but you must not touch."

Kasia fills the kettle on the stove. Her mother whimpers. Her father pets her mother's arm. Her sisters dress paper dolls. Her brothers belly-scoot in the cool barren dirt beneath the shanty, her brothers who will be made to go down into the mine when they are older, to crouch in dirty water in the wet rooms, to crawl like worms in the low rooms. Kasia tells them they should play in the woods while they can. They ignore her.

"Your mother feels stronger today," her father says.

"Strong enough to walk a few steps?" Kasia says.

"She wants to go to mass this evening," he says.

With her rag, Kasia wallops a fly crawling on the bed. "How will she get there?"

"In her finest," he says. "You'll iron her good dress and fix her hair."

Kasia grabs the buckets and stomps outside.

The three neighbor-beauties (honey-complexioned, partridge-plump) cross to Kasia as she walks the road. "Katarzyna, may we borrow a moment of your time," they coo, oh so polite. Why have they chosen her? These condescending girls with arms linked, grins like gashes, rose and turquoise skirts.

"Come see a note from a boy even stranger than you. Some silly little Italian. Swimming after us two days ago when we waded our side of the river."

"Yesterday we found this note from him in a bottle."

"Katarzyna, see what you miss now that you live as your mother's drudge!"

One holds the muddy bottle; one pulls out the plug of moss; one unrolls the wrinkled note. Kasia names him the sea swimmer. She wants time to examine the evidence of him, the green smell of the moss, the smooth glass, the particulars of his ink and paper, his handwriting, his name.

But the neighbor-girls whisk away moss and bottle and note, conceal them in pockets, laugh and glide away. Kasia does not belch, or oink, or squawk—any of these they might expect. She merely nods at them, continues walking to the pump, serene as you please, the empty bucket bumping her thigh.

But oh, she is desperate to meet the sea swimmer. His skin is golden, she is sure of that already. Once he traveled with a carnival, she surmises, and he submerged himself in a glass tank and held his breath so long the spectators went wild, men fainted from imitating him, and women sobbed because they thought he was dead. The West Fork of the Monongahela is the wrong body of water for him, stranded in landlocked West Virginia when he belongs to the sea. Or a sandy island he could invite her to, a lighthouse for them to live in, clams and starfish to catch.

Kasia's mother perches on the edge of the bed, feet wide apart, nightdress rucked up past her knees, head drooping.

Her father motions for Kasia. "She wants to practice kneeling," he says. "For when the priest says the prayers."

Her mother digs fingers into Kasia's elbow. Her father grunts. Like a rusted hinge creaking open, her mother rises. Kasia stumbles. She plants her feet wide, matching her mother's stance.

"A little more, easy, that's my girl, easy now," her father coaxes. Her mother expels a ragged breath.

Kasia knows that her own breaths are ragged too. She is already too much like her mother, unruly hair and squinting eyes more resemblance than she can stand. Her mother squeezes her elbow, and Kasia remembers a time when her mother wasn't sick, when she threw handfuls of flour and water into a bowl, and molded the dough into whatever shapes pleased Kasia and her brothers and sisters.

Kasia strips the outer leaves from the cabbage. Her brothers are outside, plucking the wings from grasshoppers; her father dozes in his chair; her mother sits up, watches her sisters show off their paper dolls.

"Kasia, I need you. Use the scissors for me," her mother says.

Kasia brings her mother the scissors from the sewing box.

Her mother shakes her head. "My fingers are too swollen. You cut slits in the heads of their dolls. So they can wear hats."

Her mother's lips stick together when she talks. Kasia accidentally cuts off half of a doll's head. Her sisters howl.

Meanwhile, plans flash through Kasia's mind. Contrive a speech to charm the bottle away from the neighbor-girls? Humble herself at their mothers' doors, beg for bones, rags, old glass? Wait for them to go to mass with their families, then break in and rifle through their things?

Kasia returns the scissors to the sewing box, the sewing box to the shelf her sisters can't reach. She takes the pan of cabbage off the stove. Her father still dozes. Her mother's eyes are closed again.

Her sisters cry, "Put her head back on! You killed her. Make a hat-slit for this one."

Kasia says, "Stop that bawling. You'll wake them."

She walks downhill, crosses the railroad tracks, turns before the bridge, follows a path of trampled weeds upriver.

Then she sees him. Slick as a tadpole, elbows and shoulder-blades and ears sticking out. The boy trembles at the edge of the river, clasping his knees with his arms, drenched, skinny, his shirt yellowed from the gritty water, so thin she can count his ribs and the knobs of his spine. His hair drying in tufts. He twitches his shoulders, spits river-water. His teeth chatter, though the July heat has already made Kasia sweat, the hair at her temples curling like two puffs of frayed rope.

"Where's your bright dress?" He springs from the ground, stands before her. "And your friends?" A bumblebee frets the air between them.

Kasia plucks her dingy dress away from her legs. "Italian?" she says.

"I lived in Calabria when I was young," he says.

"My neighbors are good Polish girls," she says. "Their mothers would shave them bald if they talked to a boy like you. And set fire to their pretty dresses, and fill their mouths with stones."

Kasia's parents don't like Italians. Most of the coal camp occupies the hills across the river from them—the company store, the doctor's office, the Italian and Polish churches and the Presbyterian, the houses of the superintendents, the huts of the Americans, the Italians, some Poles, and a few Turks. But

Kasia's family lives on the same side of the river as the mine, so that their only neighbors will be other Poles.

"What about your mother?" he says.

"Doesn't leave her bed," she says.

"And your father?"

"Doesn't leave her side."

"Are you sure?" His eyes burn through her. "Won't you lose your hair and your clothes and your voice if you talk to me?"

"I'll throw my mother's scissors in the river, and steal my sister's dress, and spit the stones at my father."

They sit down in willow shade, dip their feet in the river.

"When we crossed the ocean, the sea made me vomit, but it dazzled me too," he says. "I loved watching the waves."

"I couldn't sleep when we first got here." She moves closer, bumps her knee against his knee. "My father said I missed the rocking of my bed, the slapping of waves."

He matches his hand to her hand, palm-to-palm, fingers resting against fingers. "My father sleeps all the time cause mining wears him out. My mother has to rub his hand to wake him. I'm a trapper boy."

"My mother puts a pillow on my father's face to muffle his snores."

"My mother digs wild garlic from the woods in the spring," he says.

"Before my mother got sick, she made us go to mass every Sunday. She pinned a card of Saint Stanislaw above the stove so he could multiply our bread and our soup if he got the notion."

They take their feet out of the river, and kneel, and turn so that their other knees also bump. They match their other hands. She concentrates on memorizing him, the alchemy of breathing in his breaths and making them hers, his crooked teeth and stub nose and sparse boy-moustache, and his irises that are amber around the pupils, turning to copper at the outer edges.

August

When her mother wakes up bellowing, Kasia sinks the needle into her thumb and bloodies the unfinished hem. Her father holds his ear close to her mother's face.

"Like it's got teeth and claws and it's chewing holes in me," she hisses.

"Kasia," her father implores. "You get the doctor." His foot is still engorged and purple from the fall of the mine-roof.

The doctor's office is across the river; Kasia runs there as hard as she can. She tells the doctor, turns, and runs back. When the doctor on horseback passes her, she detours and peeks in the river boy's window. His name is Nicolo. She treats herself to a glimpse of him sitting down for dinner with his family, his mother carrying a heavy pan, and then she resumes her homeward dash. She finds her mother quiet, the doctor almost finished, her father clutching his hands behind his back.

"False labor," the doctor pronounces. "Hunger pangs. She needs nourishment. I suggest oxtail soup, fried drop cakes, creamed turnips, custard."

Kasia thinks her heart might scurry from her chest. She puts a plate of biscuits on the table. Her sisters beg for jam, her brothers refuse to wash and come inside, her father insists on staying beside her mother. Pulse thrumming, Kasia chews a biscuit, makes herself swallow it. She still wants to believe that the baby will come, and go for all she cares, and her mother will heal, and get out of bed, and tend her father, amuse her sisters, tame her brothers, put their lives to rights again.

Another fit, this time a lukewarm simmer instead of boiling over. Her mother alternates between groans and forced-out breaths, does not move, and her father says, "Kasia," and nothing more because she knows what to do now. He has wrapped his foot in all the rags he can find; he says he has less pain, but his movements are slow and lurching.

Kasia tells the doctor, "My mother's having a baby, she needs help," and then she whirls around and runs off, detouring again. Nicolo is in his front yard, rolling a barrel-hoop with his brothers. He sees her. He runs past her, runs down the mud road to distance himself from his hut and his family, and then he waits for her. He whispers that his mother might welcome her but his father would rage. She asks if he's glad she came. He holds his finger over her mouth. He gives her a penny to add to her crate of keepsakes.

Home just in time, she hears the doctor tell her father, "Only constipation. Make sure she has plenty to drink." Her father tugs his beard, chews his lip. Her mother snores.

Dog days, the muddy roads blister and crack, the river curdles. The sun looks like a fevery canker sore. Worms throng and nibble to curlicue the vines at the water-pump. A starling nests in the eaves and gives them a concert of gargling. Kasia wants to kill it, and also the ribby mongrel found and fawned over by her sisters, now hiding from them beneath the shanty. They wish to fatten, bathe, and brush, though the dog snarls, warns them to keep away. Her brothers bring sticks, good for fetching if the dog decides to play, or for poking if it hesitates.

"She can't hold food down, or drink, or breathe right. You go. I can't remember the English words the doctor would need me to say." Her father looks worse than her mother: sallow, unrested, crescents of shadow under his eyes. Filthy bandages encase his foot.

"My brave girl," her mother says, stroking her arm. "Think of some names for your new sister."

Kasia alerts the doctor and lets him trot past her as before, and then she slinks off to Nicolo's, crouches beneath his window. He comes to her, and walks her to the end of his road, all the way to the bridge, over the river, up the hill to the start of her road. Kasia wants to keep walking, but then Nicolo says, "Maybe your mother needs you," and she pushes him away.

The doctor is already gone when Kasia gets home. "He works on her two minutes, and for this I get charged!" her father fumes, pointing to her mother's belly as if Kasia could possibly forget. "He does this to us cause we're Polish. She's been pregnant ten months, if the baby gets any bigger, she might burst."

"I can't understand you when you talk so fast," Kasia says.

Her father flings up his arms. "Cause you're forgetting the tongue of your homeland, that's why. What took you so long? I couldn't make out half of what he said. I can't count on you to run for me, or translate. Next time, I go myself."

So much rain, the roof leaks at every seam. Kasia marshals her brothers and sisters to set out pans and bowls to catch the drips. Her mother screams, dozes, screams again. Her father tells her sisters to sit with their mother and keep her company, tells her brothers to build a big fire in the stove.

And then so much bloody water pours from her mother, the mattress fills like a sponge, and pinkish liquid dribbles onto the floor. Her father rams his feet into his boots, hobbles toward the door, too reckless, bends his bad foot backwards. He sits on the floor, cradles his foot, whimpers like a dumb beast.

Kasia says, "Let me go."

"My angel," her father says, still staring at his foot.

The night is black, the mud road is slick, and the rain stings. She trips as she crosses the railroad tracks, tears her dress, strikes her forehead on the fishplate. Wind knocked out of her, she tries to run again, feels too woozy. She decides she can drag herself to Nicolo's. And then he will run the rest of the way for her, and maybe his mother will offer her tea or dry things to wear, and Nicolo's father be damned.

Home again. Instead of the doctor, an Italian midwife has come, bringing silver shears and a bag of herbs. Her mother mewls like a baby bird.

"You're a mess," her father says. "And what'd you send her for?"

"Nicolo must have thought she'd be better than the doctor."

"I knew it!" her father crows. "Your mother dying in childbirth, and what do you do? Sneak off to your dirty Italian boyfriend, roll around with him, get your head bruised."

Her brothers and sisters stare at him.

"Clear out. I got to have a word with Kasia." He waves them away like he's shooing flies. Then he hits her, three slaps to her face, then a punch to her shoulder.

To show what a monster he is, Kasia overreacts, caterwauls, reels across the room when he punches her, bumps the shelf that holds her mother's dishes. Cups and bowls shatter against the floor.

Her father comes after her again, his hand raised, but then he gives up. His bad foot unsteadies him; he's drained from waiting for the baby, from the cycles of excitement and deflation, all those times thinking her mother was about to give birth.

Kasia thinks she could knock him over, if she wanted to.

The dead baby, with feathery eyelashes and cap of black hair, looks so perfect, and peaceful, and blue. Her father snugs it in his arms, paces back and forth. Her mother sleeps, her breaths smooth and even. The midwife told Kasia that if her mother lived until morning, her chances would turn for the good. And left two corncakes, told Kasia to soften them in cups of tea when her mother was strong enough to eat.

In the back room, her brothers and sisters take turns singing to her littlest sister, who won't stop crying. Kasia crawls under the shanty, sweet-talks the dog, drenched and shivering from the sideways rain. She swears she will give it beef bones, tells other lies, lets it snuffle and lick her hand. She backs up; the dog crawls toward her. Her knees sink in the mud. She tells the dog she will give it a rope of sausage five feet long, and it follows her a little more. Finally, Kasia lures it inside. The dog darts across the floor; instead of showing her sisters affection, the dog hides beneath their bed.

She thinks of other promises, these also for the good of her family. That she will leave her parents at her next chance, but not if she must marry and turn out a flock of live, dead, and half-formed babies. That she will hire herself out as a maid, or clerk at the company store, and give wages to her father and mother, and help her brothers and sisters with their lessons.

Kasia sorts some of the fragments of her mother's dishes, figures out which pieces fit together, ties all the pieces of a bowl in one rag, the pieces of a saucer in another. She sets them aside, lacking the glue to finish the job.

Then Kasia sits in her father's chair. She washes the tear-smudges from her mother's cheeks, pale as sunken bread dough. She washes her mother's soiled hands, tucks stray hairs behind her mother's ears. Brings the sheet from her own bed, tucks it around her mother, boils water to launder her mother's spattered sheet. Watches her mother, prays over her, says that if her mother strengthens while she sleeps, she'll do her part. She bides with her.

THE SINKS OF GANDY

Rulina is walking through the snow. When she reaches the frozen creek, she leans her rifle against a tree. She hears what she cannot see: the ring of water that's flowing under milky ice, tumbling over stones, then the softer notes as it passes over mud. She kneels and rolls up her sleeve, punches a hole in the ice-sheet that lids the creek, and dips her arm in. The dark water pulls at her, chills her blood, and makes her tremble, and needles her body with stars of pain.

She wriggles her fingers around, feels the ooze at the bottom of the creek. No winter cress she might gather, no mats of creek lettuce.

She walks ten paces downstream, gets down on her knees and punches another hole, dips her arm, finds nothing; she walks and punches again.

When her fingers are too stiff and cold for a fist, she pounds the ice with the flat of her hand. This time, the ice is too thick. The creek refuses her, will not open. She holds her ear to the ice, can't hear anything. Creek without tongue, without flow.

Rulina worries about her children as she walks through the snow and tries not to stumble, as she cradles the rifle, as she pounds the ice. A freckled boy who's three and does his best to help her with chores; then another boy, a reckless table-climber who gets into everything and has eyes of slate blue and carroty hair; and last, a tiny pale girl who's been slow to gain weight. Rulina left all three of them under the scrap quilt in the big straw bed, had pulled her own best wool stockings up their cold legs, had stuffed rags and corn shucks in their clothes because she knew how unbearably cold the log house could get.

She had fed them more than she should have, and she had packed most of the powder and shot, and for their fevers she had given the boys tea steeped from the last joe-pye weed. They were running out of everything. She had told her boys in her cheeriest voice what her mother had told her: Joe Pye was an Indian medicine man who cured a blacksmith's daughter with joe-pye weed, and the blacksmith was so grateful, he said he would give Joe Pye a farm, but Joe Pye didn't want it. Rulina had not told her boys the rest of what her mother had said: Joe Pye knew that men sometimes tell wicked lies, offer good things to set a trap.

No sun in the grey sky, and no ramps on the hillside, and no green nubs of trout lily in the woods in the few places where the ground is bare, without snow. Rulina would eat the pink flowers off a Judas tree, would bring her babies a clump of Solomon's-seal. It's the end of March, but winter will not take its cold grey hands off them. Under the ice-crusted beeches, she sees nothing green, not one stem or stalk. And no animal tracks, no cone middens, no piles of scat.

Rulina tries to befriend a blue jay pecking a bank of snow. She hunkers down, holds out her hand, and offers it bits that she tears from a bread-heel. The jay takes the bits, then a pearl of lard from the pouch of food she brought. Enough for a day, maybe two, if it comes to that, if she eats small.

She steps over a section of winter-ravaged fence, some of

its worm rails sagging, some snow-snapped. She steps past the boundary trees. She lays her rifle in old snow the color of trampled flour, and then she lays herself down alongside it.

There is a shadow in her.

If she stays here in her snow bed, she could become a pillar of ice, a lump of crystals gleaming in the sun. It would be a way to leave the fevers of the log house, the food whimpers and the squalling, and sour wash, and the onion poultices smeared on the chests of the men who won't get up.

The older man is lame, filmy-eyed, with a bald head that's the shape of an egg. He sings hymns if he thinks Rulina is sad; his high thin voice sounds like the wind that blows through the cracks of the house.

The younger one is the only living son of the older, and for four years, he has been the husband of Rulina. He's got freckles all over him, and a mouthful of pleasing words that she used to repeat to herself when she was alone so that she could taste their sweetness again; he has carrot-colored hair, and long wiry arms, and warm hands that she used to reach for when she was cold at night. He used to be easy for her to love. He had been a thoughtful father to their children, had been good at growing a garden, good at trapping, stalking, trailing—until his last corn crop failed, until his gun got wet, and fired wrong, flinted his face. Since then, he's been gloomy, shiftless, a blob of jelly no matter how Rulina tries to coax him.

Dock and sorrel when spring comes, the younger told her this morning. *Eat your fill of that. I'm too worn-down to go out on a day as miserable as this.*

Father and son, and both had been married to laughing wives when Rulina first knew them. They were her family's neighbors when she was a girl, and then they moved away. And returned a few years after that, widowers who said that they had lost everything. They soon became hired hands who cleared and plowed for Rulina's father, cut firewood and busted stumps. On the first day they were out working in his fields, her father asked her sisters to carry a basket of food to them. Mary Louisa, her sullen blonde sister, groaned and said she had indigestion; Catherine, her sister with wavy brown hair, said the ground was too muddy, she was afraid she would slip and fall. Rulina told her father she would take the basket.

When she found them, the younger man was hurling stones at a cloud of pigeons roosting in an enormous chestnut tree, missing often, but bringing down some; the older was whistling while he plucked the stone-slain birds, was squatting by a pile of blue-gray feathers and heads and feet.

The two men chatted with Rulina while they built a cookfire. The older told Rulina they had figured they would need to catch their own dinner, since her father had not mentioned it, since their last employer was miserly and had never fed them much. The older said that their employer's name was Stephen Pierce. They had felled and sledded and rafted oak and walnut trees from Close Mountain because Pierce wanted more new ground to farm, and planks for the bridge he was building over the Cheat River.

The younger told Rulina he had learned to throw stones from Benjamin, one of Pierce's slaves—a big man, soft-spoken, serious, with a scar above his eye. He was skilled at slinging pebbles, and pocketknives, and axes. People stopped working and gathered to watch him bite his lip and throw at whatever his target was—squirrel, mumblety peg, cow horn, walnut stump. Benjamin never missed.

The younger said, "That bastard Pierce said he never wanted to see Benjamin again and sold him to Missouri. Maybe he was jealous, or afraid."

Rulina said, "Is that what you believe? Is there something you're not telling me?"

"Pierce bedded his wife, beat him, kept him in chains," the younger said, and for the first time he looked at Rulina, as if he was taking stock. "He treated everyone like dogs."

"Was Pierce bad to you too?" Rulina said. "Is that why you moved back here?"

"I can't stand a man who's cruel," the younger said.

When the older and the younger slept in her father's barn, Rulina would rise early and go out, and they would call down to her from the haymow while she milked the brindle cow. She liked the froggy voice of the younger one, the sweet and husky way he said her name, how he shared with her reports about the swallows who had hatched their chicks in the eave. And she liked the gentle voice of the older one, his sunny mood, his habit of singing to himself as he worked.

One day, the older surprised Rulina: he looked at her with devouring eyes and told her he was ready to marry again, that she would find he was mild as a spring lamb. Rulina knew enough to distrust what he was claiming, and she tried to avoid him after that.

The younger one had started watching Rulina too, and she thought he had kind eyes, a bashful smile, and so she turned her thoughts to him. She stood close to him when she thought he wouldn't notice. She liked the warmth of him, his rich smell; even in the summer, she could smell on him the woods on a snowy day, and the deer skins he tanned with the bark of buck oaks, and the spruce needles he slept in when he hunted, and the fires he built when he had to sleep on cold ground.

She asked her sisters what they thought of him. They said they thought he was suitable. Mary Louisa said, "You don't want one who's bald, hairy, warted, sniveling, too soft, too rough." Catherine said, "Or one like his father."

In the summer, the younger surprised Rulina by attending the love feast at the Dunkard meetinghouse where Rulina's father was an elder; he had never gone with them before. Rulina fixed him a plate of beef and apple butter and pickles; they talked a while, and he told her that he had been praying, reading the Gospel of John, and examining his heart. He sat at the brothers' table—next to her father, away from Rulina and the sisters' table—and so Rulina couldn't see him during the footwashing, the passing of the holy kiss, the sharing of the cup. After the service, Rulina walked home beside him. He didn't say much, but she thought she could see tears on his face.

Outside her father's barn, the younger said, "You would be a fine wife." He was looking at his feet, had his hands clasped behind his back.

That night, Rulina decided she would say yes to the younger. She felt fortunate when she thought about all the chance things that had worked to bring them together: her father needed a field hand, and the younger wanted a benevolent employer, and her sisters would not carry food to him. Rulina thought he would be good and steadfast and honest, unlike the older. And he was, for a while.

She remembered what the younger had promised her. He said he had borrowed and bought a good farm with a sound log house and plenty of everything—not too far from Seneca Flats, where she would find a Presbyterian church and a trade post that'd have what she needed.

Maybe he meant that the farm would be good someday if they worked for it, struggled for it. The farm is thickly treed, in a hollow, below a sharp boulder-strewn ridge Rulina will never cross. The log house is in shadows most of the day, Rulina has discovered; she tacks up old skins to keep the wind out; she has a dirt floor, smoky chimney, hickory table, clothes pegs, cedar buckets, earthen pots, not much else.

Plenty of everything, he said. Such a gulf between what is spoken and what is understood. When Rulina walks on the farm, she sifts his words, tries to make them fit what she sees: plenty of swamp and water snakes and mosquitos, and plenty of steep land, and hawthorns that tear her hands, and greenbriers that trip her and stick to her sleeves.

The younger told her that he would need to fell oaks for new ground and burn the lesser trees right away. If he had more hours in the day, he would make a deadening—a patch of slow-failing trees he could clear away a few years from now. "Let me help you," Rulina said. She meant, I want us to work together. She knew she would be sweaty, dirty, sore—but it would be bearable because they were sharing the labor.

The younger said, "I won't refuse you." He walked with her to the ground he was working, pointed out the raw stumps, the tangles of uprooted brush, the burn heap. And then he took her to another part of the farm—over a steep pine hill, through yet another swamp, a good twenty minutes away. "You can work here," he said. "Watch me girdle this one." He swung his axe, showed her how to chip away a wide collar of bark from one tree, then another. He watched her swing a few times, and kissed her, and left her to make the deadening by herself. She didn't question him. She told herself this might be another kind of working together. She found that she liked the weight of the axe in her hands, the bark chips and sapwood flakes piling at her feet, the groan of the trunk when she struck it, the echo of the groan coming back to her. Sometimes she hollered, and her echo sounded familiar but also strange, like the voice of a twin she had forgotten, a spirit that had roamed and was now returning.

After that, when Rulina was pregnant and couldn't work outside as much, the younger invited the older to stay in the log house with them. He gave Rulina more false promises. *For a few weeks, maybe a month. He's got bad leg pains. He spilled hot fat on his foot. Maybe he can stay a little and help us clear.* She told herself the younger was a generous son, and this invitation must be part of his goodness. Soon, she learned that there was no getting away from the clamor and the mess that the two of them made. The older hooted and brayed, cursed his leg as he limped around. He no longer pretended that his was a gentle voice. He and the younger shouted for each other and slammed around all day, and cleared their throats and spat with gusto, and told jokes that resulted in snorts, guffaws, table-banging.

Although they are quieter now that they won't get up from their bearskins near the fire, the younger still snores at night, tosses and flails. And now he coughs too. And the older has nightmares sometimes, screams like a panther in his sleep, then wakes up and cries for water. *To cool my tongue,* he says.

And Seneca Flats is seven miles away, not nearby; when Rulina had gotten there, newly married and with a list of things she wanted to buy, she saw that the church was boarded up, and there was little sign of people, and the trade post was a shack with a leaky roof and empty shelves. She didn't go again.

In her snow bed—broken fence behind her, rifle within reach— Rulina thinks about Gandy Creek. It loops like unspooled thread, then runs through a valley that's deep and narrow and blind. When it has nowhere else to go, the creek sinks into the mouth of a cave. Like a lost river, nobody knows how long, running for miles and miles underground.

In her dreams, she has no other path, nowhere else to go. She chooses the creek; she runs with it into the rocky mouth; she sinks with it under the earth. Her shoes off, her skirts pulled up. The creek is a warm surging thing, and it does not freeze her. She passes through a chamber where hundreds of bats hang from the ceiling like scraps of shadow, like flowers folded in on themselves, their wings stirring and stirring even as they dream.

The creek is a dark ribbon that she follows by tallow-light. And in that ribbon, there is her mortal body wading downstream. Mirrored behind her, there is her reflection, a body of shimmer that minnows pass through, minnows so pale she sees the trace of blood vessels. Vessels like red spider-legs, like red smoke, the branching of the thinnest lines. And at the creek's outflow, she pours through, and runs in the next valley, runs beyond the impassable ridge, runs through sunlight, through gold-light that spills down on everything, spills down on her, spills down on a come-alive land that is all leaf and bud, spring breeze and honeysuckle scent, bird song and frog song.

Rulina rises too fast, wobbles, waits a moment for the strength to return to her numb legs, for the feeling of pins and needles to fade from her cold hands.

She shakes out her skirts, her sleeves, and follows Gandy Creek upstream, away from the sinks. Flakes are falling, easy for a while, then whirling before her, fat and wet. Patches of old snow crunch under her feet as she works her way uphill; the woods thicken, then grow sparse. A loud noise startles her— maybe a snort, or a gasp. She stiffens, and plants her feet, and holds her breath.

She hears the feathery sound of snow-siftings, then thuds that could be footfalls.

Something shakes a spruce tree. She sees an antler tip. A flared nostril. A bull elk traipses into view, and stops in front of the tree, and browses the spruce limbs. First she's seen in seven years. Maybe the last. The men think that the buffaloes are gone, the beavers are gone, the elk are probably gone too, although there was a rumor of a bony yearling elk seen on the road last winter. This one's a rare and lordly beast, lordly the way he holds his head and great antlers. Long-legged, thick in the chest. The snowy trees diminish behind him. Rulina smells the strong musk of him. His undercoat is like wool, his tail and rump-patch a creamy yellow, his neck-mane and winter shag the deep brown of walnut dye.

The bull elk returns her stare with large, fierce eyes, and then he grunts, shakes his head, and browses again, as if he is no longer curious about her. His antlers, nearly as tall as he, curve like the prow of a ship.

Rulina stares at the antlers and tries to follow the maze of branches and tines, and then she feels dizzy. She remembers sleeping in the deep spruce needles with the younger when he was teaching her to hunt, how warm she was when he curled around her. She remembers cringing the first time she shot a squirrel, and cringing again later that day when the older handed her the skinning knife, the whetstone, and then the hammer. She asked what the hammer was for, and the older laughed, told her she that after she was done with skinning and singeing, she would have to pound and pound the squirrel-bodies until the bones were crushed to fine splinters, until the meat was a soft pulp.

She remembers feeding her babies watery gravy, and corn-cakes thin as paper, and roots scrawny and colorless.

She bites her cool lip. Maybe the last day they'll be hungry, maybe the day the younger turns for the better, the day when her boys' fevers break and pink comes to her daughter's cheeks and she drives the cold away, the day when she reaches for the younger's hands and there is love again.

She aims at his shoulder. The rifle booms, and his blood sprays out as the rifle-kick staggers Rulina into the snow. She lifts her head, sees the elk leaping up and running a few yards, and then he struggles, then he crumples to his knees. A cloud of steam rises from his great brown body.

Rulina grabs a leg, strains, and shoves, and gets the bull elk onto his side. Too heavy for her to hang, and she has no rope.

His antlers snag in the galax-vines. She'll need to return with a saw, maybe an axe. With her knife, she cuts rings around his legs, cuts him from the breastbone down, careful not to pierce the guts. She starts to peel the skin, gets some of it off, stops trying—she's so weary, and she's further from home than she meant to be, and she wants them to have plenty to eat. She takes from him his tongue, heart and liver, pieces of loin, hunks of flesh that she cuts into long strings. She turns for home with her apron full of meat.

The men will not get up from their pallets at the hearth when Rulina returns. Her babies cheeping like birds, fire almost out, the men sharing a dirty blanket, and Rulina with blood in her hair, freighted with all the meat she can carry.

In the months to come, she will chink the log house with clay and little stones and elk hair. And when her babies whimper and she can't soothe them, when her milk dries up, when the garden struggles, new potatoes no bigger than peas, she will have some elk meat that she's salted and hung and dried in the sun, that's she hidden away. She will have her picture of the underground creek, running and running beneath the shell of the earth, sinking and sinking before it pours out again.

JUNE DROP

Winesap

As he walks to his car, Riley peels off his sweater, thinking that the first week of March shouldn't be as hot as the first week of summer. One more thing that puts knots in his stomach. He drives across town. When he sees a sign propped against the guardrail, *Produce and Flea Market*, red spray paint on plywood, Riley cuts a hard left and angles into the parking lot. He quarreled with Stephanie this morning, he'll be late if he doesn't hurry, he'll be in hot water. He thinks of the word *unseasonable*. Although he keeps hoping love will grow, maybe it's the wrong time for both of them. He should tell her it isn't working, he's tired, he's had enough, he wants out.

Or he could bring Stephanie a peace offering. And a present for Clint; he likes to think he would do anything for Stephanie's kid.

An old man peers down at a card table jumbled with salt-shakers, souvenir spoons, a toaster studded with magnets, and snow globes, ceramic vases, bottle openers shaped like lobsters and crabs. An old woman is selling embroidered potholders, jars of sauerkraut, shelled walnuts, rows of apples. The apples are small, misshapen, dull yellow. The word *produce* has made Riley want something green, lush, growing, full of sap and vitality. Instead, here are two junk dealers, him in coveralls, her in sweatpants and a sleeveless top patterned with rosebuds.

"Ever taste a Winesap, young man?" She quarters an apple,

offers him a wedge. Riley tastes it, although he would rather turn from her and count backward, or flee to his car, dodging strangers, chit-chat, potential entanglements.

It's tart, then sweet, then tart again, and a cool gray cellar comes to Riley in a flash, bins that store apples like these, gnarled trees on a hill, and the working together of sun and rain, the mix of worry and hope in waiting for a crop, the hands that tended and harvested, mentholatum and heat rub for sore joints. Riley takes a deep breath and says, "I'll buy a basket."

She says, "Gerald, he needs half a peck."

It takes a moment for her request to sink in, for Gerald to stop gazing at the spoons, put down his polish rag, walk stiffly over to their truck.

For once, Riley wants to say something; for once, what he says doesn't fizzle, backfire, or dead-end. "Would these apples be good for a mother and her son?"

The basket is lined with a plastic bag, and as Gerald lifts it out, he winks at Riley and says, "Ask Lottie."

Lottie tells Riley, "Pick that gal a potholder she'll like."

Riley drives away, but then he stops again at a boarded-up gas station, unknots the bag, curls his hand around a Winesap, and breaks the skin with his teeth.

A Little Off the Top

Riley knows what kind of day Stephanie's had by the dessert she chooses. Nonfat whipped topping and peaches in light syrup if she's happy, playful. Watermelon cubes if she wants to pick a fight, spit watermelon seeds so hard he can hear them hit the trashcan with angry pings.

If he wants to know more, he picks up the comb and scissors in her salon. He learns about people from smell, touch, and taste. *Tuning in,* he calls it. Discussing it with people is hard, even with Stephanie. Sometimes tuning in is handy, letting him gauge a person's attitude or motives, but it can be bothersome, come on him in waves. And when impressions bombard him, he breathes faster, his hands get clammy, he'd rather just stay home. Restaurants unnerve him. Stephanie doesn't ask him to take her out anymore.

When he handles her comb, he catches a trace of worry, her jitters on the first day of beauty school, then the first time she was paid for cutting hair. Even now she's always anxious, trying hard to make each customer look good. She keeps a special comb and scissors for family and friends. These feel different somehow. The plastic is warmer; the metal drones, then hums, and Riley knows that Stephanie hums when she trims Clint's hair, that she would shield him from all pain if she could. She can't win with Clint's teachers, no matter how often she complains, and she can't bring up his reading level, or stop the bus bullies who hound him.

When Riley leans back in the styling chair, she hums, pins a towel over his shoulders and rakes her fingers through his shaggy brown hair. Even when he doesn't want a haircut, he lets her take a little off the top because she follows the haircut with a facial and scalp massage, and he likes cucumber slices on his eyes, her fingers on the nape of his neck.

Reminder

Don't forget her lip balm, don't buy the wrong brand. Riley keeps repeating these words in his head. Sometimes, a thought gets stuck like the paper in the adding machine at the used bookstore where he works. It was easier when he and Stephanie both lived in Belington, but then she moved to Webster Springs to live in her cousin's spare house, where she does hair and manicures in the living room she's christened *the salon.*

Driving those seventy-four miles between her house and his, buzzed on anticipation or on a good visit just concluded, or in a funk, a slump, a haze, he cranks up his Joan Baez tapes. Today, he chooses the slow route, through Mill Creek and Elkwater, so that he can follow the long serpentine ridge of Point Mountain and have the road to himself. A light rain falls. He glances over the rusty guardrails and tries to see down the wooded slopes into the deep valleys far below, the fields of giant boulders and sinkholes.

He finds the farm stand near Cherry Falls. The rain is steadier now. Along with junk and produce tables, Gerald and Lottie have set up a homemade pavilion that shelters a gas grill and a picnic table. Gerald is painting a bird cage; Lottie is stirring a soup pot. Lottie asks, did his friend like the apples he bought her. Riley knows that unless he intervenes, the apples will meet a ghastly end in Stephanie's fridge, where lemons grow fur and salad mix rots to puddles of slime.

Lottie lids the pot and says, "I hope she made you a pie."

Riley looks at his hands, can't think of what he should say. All he sees is the smear on his palm where he inked the word *chapstick* when he left the bookstore two hours ago.

Pinto Beans

Riley buys soup beans and a pickled beet from Lottie. He chews slowly, nods at Lottie when she talks. Each bite makes him feel hungrier, more hollow, unfillable. "So good," he says.

"You have to soak pintos all night, simmer them all day," Lottie says.

The bean broth is thick, flecked with ramps and sausage, even better with crumbled cornbread. Lottie talks about their daughters, then their neighbors who used to raise a dozen kinds of apples, now she and Gerald have the last orchard. The soup beans tell Riley a lot about them, he knows or he guesses that Gerald still butchers a hog every fall, and Lottie's right there with a scraper, spatters of blood, rubber boots and dark purple entrails, they use every bit. And he believes that Lottie cooks without recipes, estimates instead of measures, follows her instincts.

Riley asks her if she can wrap some peach cobbler for him to take. Gerald shows them a round tray he's been buffing. The left side of his face sags, looks a little melted, like a candle left too long in the sun; the fingers of his left hand are claw-like. He flips his good hand so that Riley sees a circle of dark tarnish, then a circle of shine.

Pocketknife

A few weeks later, on another rainy day, Riley finds the farm stand relocated again, near Hacker Valley on a crescent of gravel between the road and Holly River. Gerald has been fishing. Lottie greets Riley, fixes him a plate of boiled new potatoes and buckwheat pancakes with rhubarb sauce. Gerald sits down to shed his hip-waders. Riley sees a sign on the picnic table, *Orchard Hand Wanted, Grafting, Beetle Removal*, magic marker on a cardboard tent.

"I think I could help," Riley says.

"Weekends would be good," Lottie says. "Do you have any experience?" Then she goes to wait on a woman in a rain poncho who's ready to buy a carton of radishes.

Riley is supposed to attend a cookout at Stephanie's cousin's place on Saturday, *bring a covered dish and your dancing shoes*. He dreads the chaos of backyard volleyball and the spray of kicked sand, holding her purse while she dances with other men, and the complex intimacy of the buffet table, the care that went into each finger food, side dish, and dessert, the interpersonal nuances of who among the partygoers takes helpings of what and how much.

"I could work for you," Riley says. "Starting Saturday."

Gerald goes to a table, paws through a box of screwdrivers and soup spoons, finds a pocketknife that he gives to Riley.

"Was this yours?" Riley says. From the knife's weight in his hand, he figures that Gerald owned it, that its meaning has changed over the years.

"My uncle's, then my son's," Gerald says, his voice slow and wobbly. "He was in the service."

Lottie tells Gerald, "Someone wants to offer you five dollars for that bird cage."

Uncle, nephew who became a father, son, father again, Riley tunes in as he drives away, never taking his eyes off the twisty road, the sheets of rain, the sky striated and ominous. His windshield wipers tick while the knife pulses in his hand. Farmer, field hand, soldier on deployment, orchard keeper. Acres planted and fence that's new, and ears of corn, muddy ditch, puddles, convoy of tactical trucks, berms across the road, barbed wire, ambush, kill sack, and oil wells burning, smoke that dims the sun, wetlands drained, city invaded by tanks, oil poured into the sea, ruined water, ruined sky, and slot in the ground, varnished box, crisp flag—and then Riley loses his glimpse of Gerald's son. He thinks he sees leaves, blossoms, a circle of trees that endures frost, and aphids, and summer scorch.

June Drop

Gerald and Lottie's farm is nine miles up a dirt road. They show Riley their former orchard first, its apples few and mealy, its trees arthritic, cracked, gray as ghosts. Then they take him to the new orchard of dwarf and semi-dwarf trees, where marble-sized apples fall around them. Riley forgets about the cookout that Stephanie is going to without him. He can feel something pass in the air, a transference or exchange, the world coming to balance again, a little bubble of hope, the feeling that everything's right, even while his shoulders are pelted by the falling apples. He thinks he'll have bruises.

Riley's good feeling doesn't last. Lottie tells him that the falling apples are the June drop, meaning some baby apples are shed so that the fruit that's still on the trees can continue to mature.

"But this is May," he says. "Not June."

"The drop comes earlier every year," Gerald says.

"I heard something on the radio," Lottie says in a low voice. She leans on her cane. "They think apples are going to quit turning red. And it could be sooner than you think."

And then the world is topsy-turvy again, and Riley sees a globe with no more ice caps, no more blue water, a ball of fire, oceans clotted with swirls of oil, plastic trash, sea turtles snarled in six pack rings, no more snow leopards or spider monkeys— and then he makes himself stop, he pinches his hand, he doesn't want to see what Clint has done to survive in that awful place.

Yellow Transparent

Riley finds the door locked, rattles the knob. Clint lets him in. "Mom went to get a pizza," he says, handing Riley an orange crayon. They color lumberjacks and dinosaurs, play crazy eights and Battleship, an hour, two hours.

Riley spreads peanut butter on apple slices, says to Clint, "Let's have a snack."

After go fish and more crazy eights, Riley helps the boy get ready for bed, fills his plastic gorilla cup, tucks him in. Clint calls for Riley, says that he spilled the water. Riley goes to the hamper for a towel, grabs what's on top, a man's denim shirt, jerks his arm away, doesn't want to know. He can't block the man's scent, an aggressive swirl of body odor, deodorant, gasoline, the beer and chili dogs with onions the man had for lunch.

"I got cold at the fireworks last night," Stephanie says, glaring at him. "Fireworks that you decided not to go see. I wore a halter top for you, frosted my hair for you, tanned for you."

Riley is sitting on the couch, massaging her feet. He says, "Was that really for me? His smell makes me sick."

She says, "That's your problem. Cooking up all these dramas, these make-believes, working yourself up. You need to quit."

Riley squirts more coconut oil into his hand. "I brought you something," he says.

"So did I," she says. She gives him a silver cuff bracelet with Celtic knots.

She meant *special gift*, he meant *a little bit of nothing, nothing fancy*, but he gives it to her anyway. "A yellow transparent, first of the season," he says. "A Russian apple." She holds it near his nose, brings her face close to his. They look at its greenish-yellow skin, speckled with light dots, then look at each other. "They're supposed to get less sour if you wait a week. And change colors," he says.

"I can wait," she says. "For a while." He feels her breath on his face. Then she leaves him on the couch, clears the plates he left on the coffee table. Soon, he hears the bathroom door swing shut, the pipes clank as she runs the shower. Riley wonders if he should go in there, put his hand on the vinyl curtain, find out if there's any further trace of Stephanie's shirt-loaning man for him to tune in.

Fourteen-Day Pickles

Riley works in the orchard a few times a week. On rainy days, Gerald asks him to work inside the barn, then inside the house.

Riley sees cucumbers everywhere: piled on the table, the counters, the sideboard. Five more buckets of cucumbers stand by the back door. The kitchen smells earthy, and clean, and alive. Riley scrubs cucumbers in the sink, Gerald quarters them long-ways, Lottie stands them in stone jars and covers them with boiling salt water. Riley can hear Lottie singing faintly. *Wish I had a needle and thread, fine as I could sew. I'd sew her to my side, down the road we'd go.*

"She stole this recipe," Gerald says.

"Riley doesn't want to hear it," says Lottie, wiping her face with her apron.

"She couldn't cook when we got married," he says.

"That's not the way to start that story," Lottie says as she arranges cucumber spears. "My grandmother had a hard life. She had only three things that anyone wanted. The first was, she could work like a man, could put out a huge garden, chop wood, right until the end when she got sick and I went to live with her. The second thing was a giant old Bible with brass hinges. And she had this pickle recipe. She left it to my sister Pearl, who gave her trinkets and candy, acted real cozy, but never lived with her." Lottie measures salt into her hand, adds it to the brine.

"She stole this recipe," Gerald says to Riley.

"Not so," Lottie insists. "I just peeked when it was left in plain view."

Riley goes to the attic, brings down a milk jug filled with vinegar that Gerald pressed last fall, then goes outside and snips handfuls of the dill that grows unbidden near the springhouse. Lottie says she'll re-boil the brine each day for the next two weeks. Riley measures, then mixes the vinegar and dill with sugar, alum, cloves, and peppercorns. Lottie shows him how.

Pool Party

Riley tells himself he'll go with Stephanie the next time there's a cookout or some other occasion, he wants to be there for her, even if it's difficult. He says he'll go to a pool party for a boy's birthday. Stephanie gives him a big kiss, says the party will be friendly, not overwhelming, he might be the only guy, no big deal if he stands off by himself and people-watches.

It's an in-ground pool with a diving board, a brilliant turquoise kidney bean. Four moms, four boys, and Riley. Stephanie and the other moms wear bikini tops and beach wraps, have no desire to go in the water. "I haven't had a good tanning day for weeks," Stephanie says. Riley helps her coat Clint with sunscreen until he gleams like a buttered cookie sheet.

When Clint won't even stick his big toe in, Riley knows what he'll have to do. He takes his shirt off, shows Clint how to ease into the pool via the ladder, promises him the water isn't deep, it feels good. Although he's wearing jean shorts, Riley doesn't feel as foolish as he thought he would. Clint steps off the ladder and hurls himself at Riley, churns up spray that burns Riley's eyes, kicks him, loops an arm around his neck and tugs on his silver chain so that the sun-charm digs into his collarbone. Somehow, Riley stays on his feet, doesn't topple.

"Can I tell you a secret?" Riley says.

Clint rolls his eyes. "You're afraid of the water, afraid of everything," Clint says.

So much for reassuring him. Still, he lets Riley give him a piggyback ride to the middle of the pool.

Water Wings

Stephanie reminds Riley of some elegant bird as she glides through her first dinner at Lottie and Gerald's. She says all the right things, laughs when Gerald tells a joke about a turkey and a tractor. And she laughs again when he tells the same joke ten minutes later, and she murmurs appreciatively as she tastes Lottie's fried chicken, potato salad, tomato slices, applesauce, and buttermilk. Clint's manners are perfect too—napkin in his lap, please and thank you—and Stephanie beams at him, washcloth-scrubbed and hair-spiked-up, her charming little man.

But Riley also catches Stephanie wrinkling her nose when Gerald offers them mint-flavored toothpicks, when Lottie slides a rubber band around her messy bun of hair. Whatever she glances at turns to shabbiness: plants in styrofoam cups on every sill; the fridge covered with calendars and paper scraps that hold Gerald's notes on the apple crop; bowls of dog kibble; mildew on the ceiling; the rust spots on the stove where Lottie painted ladybugs and zinnias.

Loading her trunk with Rome Beauties and Rusty Coats, Riley moves the goggles and armbands that Stephanie bought to help Clint learn to swim. Riley flashes on Clint convincing her to take him to the public pool so that he can practice, the determined look on Clint's face as he pinches his nose, lowers his face into the water, learns to dog paddle. *Floaties*, Clint calls the armbands.

Riley's mother gave him some when he was a boy. He wasn't afraid of the water; rather, he was embarrassed by the cartoon dinosaurs on his trunks, and his flabby belly, and the people staring at his father, who was ankle-deep in the kiddie pool, gesturing wildly. His mother was embarrassed too. His father rolled his r's and waved an invisible flag like a bullfighter, then called him "matie" in his pirate voice, urged him to wade in. It had always been that way, Riley thinks now, his father or his mother dragging him where he did not want to go, kindergarten, Sunday school, Cub Scouts, the allergy doctor, when all he wanted was the solace of his own thoughts, a library book, the quiet of his bedroom, the door shut. He had stood there at the edge of the pool, feeling like he had been ejected from solid ground, and the rainbow-colored mosaic tiles of the cement deck were a thousand far planets and he was falling, would always fall.

"I'll get you some water wings," his mother said the next day, in the privacy of their station wagon. That sounded wonderful to Riley. He wanted to believe in a device that could help him fly through the water, maybe even swim in the sky.

Blight

After months of too much rain, some of the apples turn oozy, rot on the branch, crack open, even burst apart. Gerald shows Riley leaves that look scorched, Winesaps that are weeping ooze. "The worst fire blight we've ever had," he says. On dry days, he and Riley cut the sick shoots from the trees, scrape the sick bark from the branches, dip their pruning knives in bleach water after each cut.

No Oil

In the winter, the bookstore is struggling, and Riley's hours get cut. He looks for odd jobs; he clears snow and stacks firewood for Grady, a scowling man who expects him on the job at dawn. Riley likes the cold air that pricks his face if he sheds his scarf.

And he likes getting to the sidewalks while the snow waits for him in broad white expanses, fresh and serene, not yet stamped by boots or flecked with cinders.

When Riley goes downstairs for his coffee and toast, sometimes Clint is already awake, wearing his snowsuit and two afghans, stationed at the dinette and absorbed in the Mighty Men and Monster Maker that Riley found for him in one of Gerald's flea market boxes. *Create scary monsters and superguys with a kit that'll give you the creeps.* From the assorted tiles, Clint chooses a crocodile's head, an astronaut's arms and torso, a pair of minotaur legs, and then covers them with a sheet of paper that he rubs with a crayon so the raised outlines show through.

"See if my cousin will hire you. He needs a new Santa Claus," Stephanie says, trying to provoke Riley, when she comes to bed in her flannel nightgown, leg warmers, and army socks. They can't afford another tank of oil, which makes her grouchy. They should have rationed the easy happiness of those first few weeks after he moved in.

"Screaming babies. Kids who know I'm fake and hate me for pretending. Kids who think I'm real and pin their hopes on me," says Riley. "No thanks."

Stephanie says, "Your ideal job would be a dark cubicle in a deserted building, no windows and no telephone." She reaches for Riley's hand, moves it to her shoulder.

As he presses his thumbs against her back, Riley gets a picture of a future she longs for. At first, all he tunes in is Stephanie on a chaise lounge, reading a magazine and tanning and by herself. And then he zooms in on warm gritty sand, pink shells and dark pebbles scattered at the tideline, and a slice of ocean, pale blue and miraculously clean. Then he sees wine coolers, variegated beach towels, a teenage version of Clint balancing on a surfboard, it's a vacation she's always saved for, a vacation *they've* always saved for, Riley is there too, helping Stephanie search for sea glass.

He knows it doesn't work that way, but as he touches her, he tries to send her a picture in return: a good paycheck that he'll earn somehow, Clint with a microscope and a tray of seedlings, a modest house for them in the middle of an orchard.

York Imperial

Riley calls Stephanie's cousin, gets a job as Santa's photographer. Ten feet away, he can tolerate the yowling babies, children with sticky fingers, suspicious eyes; he evades the textures of crocheted scarves and nylon jackets, the odors of cough drops and candy canes. He's managing so far, more or less. Riley works Santa's evening shift at a department store twenty-six miles away, in Summersville. He gets home late; Clint is already in bed, reading to Stephanie from one of his chapter books. Even with sentences that are mostly sight words, Clint's reading voice is shy and unsure. He'd doing better at math, he likes the karate lessons he takes twice a week (free for him because Stephanie's sister is the sensei), he wants a bongo drum for Christmas. Stephanie plans to knit a scarf for Gerald and give Lottie a coupon for a free haircut, but she tells Riley these gifts aren't enough, he'd better think of something.

Stephanie warms the salon with a space heater so her customers won't suffer. She and Riley and Clint sleep before its benevolent orange glow on the coldest nights, all three of them on mattresses on the salon floor, their chilly bodies spent and jammed close.

Out in the garage, behind Stephanie's elliptical machine and bronzing lamp, behind Clint's flying saucer sled, Riley has hidden a barrel of apples. Forty-five York Imperials, tough-skinned, yellow with patches of sun blush, picked in October before they were fully ripe. With gentle hands, Riley packed these apples in straw and corn husks, placed them snugly, cheek-to-cheek. When the time is right, he will usher Stephanie and Clint to the garage, reveal his secret, give them the Yorks. Something that's ripened in the dead and dark of winter. The fragrant smell of apples will rise from the barrel when he pries up the lid in January; maybe they will have apples the year after too. He will keep count of the days until then.

RING OF EARTH

I can begin here: remembering my grandparents on icy winter nights. When I see glimmers in the dark, bits of light, I think of their Angus cattle farm on Pea Ridge in Barbour County. I can imagine a smudge of moon, my grandfather popping corn in a skillet with bacon grease. And my grandmother stirring red coals in the furnace. And my grandfather's boot-prints in the snow, him walking over the knob, around the new pond, down into the woods where his shadow mixed with tree-shadows and you couldn't tell one from the other.

If it was Christmas Eve, she would light the Magi candle and give me a joe frogger cookie; he would play his guitar, sing "Mammas Don't Let Your Babies Grow Up to Be Cowboys." Outside, the snow would be coming down fast, sure to stick to edges and rims, sassafras and sumac, the lip of the trough, the cow bones scattered through the hickory woods. Ice would lid the old pond that shrank each year, clouding over, like an eye going blind. I can imagine my finger or nose freezing to chrome letters on the spare-parts truck, and icicles hanging from the eaves like sharp teeth.

Soon, the snow would cover my grandfather's tracks, blanket their farm, making it unfamiliar, a story written over.

I live five hundred miles away from their farm. At the aquarium in Chattanooga, I am with my older son, holding his hand. We descend the walkways that zigzag down the Secret Reef. He's three. He's not saying much. Every so often, a word. Or he makes a sound. Or he reaches his hand toward water, green turtle, hundreds of bright fish. So much to take in. I can call what I see in him *awe*. Inside the plastic observation bubble of the Undersea Cavern, we sprawl on our backs, look up at the reef, the bellies of sandbar sharks.

When he wants to see something else, we go into a plain room that holds a tank of endangered laurel dace, relocated here after drought dried up their shoestring creeks on the Cumberland Plateau. Each laurel dace is yellow-finned, orange-bellied, the size of a thumb. Scientists caught eighteen survivors with seine nets, transported them here, now maintain them as an ark population.

"Fish," the boy says.

"Fish swim," I say, try to give him an encouraging look. I'm always pleading with him to say more.

He peers back at me, but he doesn't say anything. He might be a late bloomer; he might have a language delay, or maybe some more serious problem.

At bedtime, I read to both my sons. I read *The Underwater Alphabet Book*. The baby runs his hand over the page, looking for a flap to lift. The older boy says, "More," and so I do: I read *Mike Mulligan and His Steam Shovel*. He's fascinated by bulldozers, backhoes, loaders. I read, "Mary Ann lowered the hills and straightened the curves to make the long highways."

While the boys sleep, I surf the web, read about kelp forests, gold-brown seaweeds ravaged by sea urchins, the water too warm, heating up. About the Marion 5960-M, a multi-ton stripping shovel at the River Queen Surface Mine. I read until I'm worried, my pulse quickens, something is squeezing me.

*

I pull this from the gray air word by word: hay season, I was thirteen, staying with my grandparents. My grandfather listened to the weather radio, the feed from Backbone Mountain, making sure there was little chance of rain. My grandmother and I were playing rummy 500, and he scowled at us. He told me, "Put your long pants on." He meant he wanted me to work with him outside.

In the meadow, I stepped around splats of manure; I stomped on a puffball, and it coughed up its rich brown dust. I was too scrawny to lift the bales onto the flatbed truck, but I helped my grandfather and my uncle by rolling the bales, grouping them together. Grasshoppers sprung from the hay stubble. My skin was scratched by stems, timothy heads, the rough twine.

My grandfather, my uncle, and I unloaded and stacked the bales in the stuffy hayshed, which had a warm grassy smell. I saw the mud nests of swallows, motes and seeds caught in the light that spilled between the boards. My grandfather kept tractor-parts in the hayshed, and come-alongs, buckets, pans of axel grease.

I took a bath after we were done. My grandmother gave me aloe for the scratches on my neck and arms, the thin red lines. We all sat down for supper. My grandfather was tired from putting up hay, from pouring himself out. My grandmother had cooked for us sirloin tips from their butchered steer, onions from their garden, and morels she picked under a dying tulip tree.

And then my grandfather was sick, then cancer riddled, wasted, and thinned all that he was. He gave up his chainsaw and rototiller. He became housebound, and sat by the window in his soft recliner, and counted dark-eyed snowbirds on the telephone wire.

He had chemo, remission, relapse. Finally, my grandmother

insisted that his doctors say it to her plain. Say the truth about him she had made life with, him she had known fifty years, field after field cut and raked and cured, jar upon jar of peppers and applesauce and pickles, and all the calves, and piglets, and chicks. And vines on the burn heap, and counting moons.

This might be hard to hear. He has a few weeks left. We can make him comfortable.

She moved him home, the house he had built for them. She put the railed bed in the living room with its plenty of windows, tilted it so he would see family pictures on the mantel, the dirt road that crossed Pea Ridge. So he would see the maple and peach trees, meadow, mockingbird, and their cows. If he lifted his head, if he opened his eyes. He was all bone, light as a bag of hay.

My grandmother said, "He was always a strong person, always in charge, very positive."

Now, he fretted if she went outside. He wanted her near. She let the garden go. She stayed by him, and tucked his sheets, his blanket, and dabbed his brow, and brought ice she had pounded, and held the cold shards to his lips.

She named farm animals for him, as Adam had done. Rabbit. Kingbird. Wolf spider swinging on a thread.

At six a.m., the older boy and I wake up. Before I take him to preschool, we watch the blue owl teaching math to a magic kite, Mister Rogers fixing a chair for Francois Clemmons. I think the boy knows the words for hammer and glue. He loves to repair things.

As I drive him to town, I carry on a mostly one-sided conversation. I point out *bucket truck, chicken truck, log truck.* On Inman Street, there's the carving of a Cherokee man. "Look at the wooden face," I say. I try to open the world to him whenever

we walk, naming for him *horse* and *mailbox, steeple* and *leaf*.
I'm flinging words, I'm praying against stony ground.

While my grandfather rested in the next room, my grandmother
and I ate breakfast at the kitchen table.

"Tell me about how you met him," I said. I thought it was
a story that she liked to tell.

"It was a blind date at the fair," she said, buttering the toast.
"My sister had warned me that if I went to nursing school, I
would drop out and marry a farmer from Lost Creek."

I thought about a creek that vanishes, slips under the mossy
stones, runs beneath the skin of the earth.

"Was he a farmer then?" I said.

"He was driving a power shovel, at a strip mine near Smith
Chapel. The day he came for me, he had a fresh haircut; he
put on a suit and tie. In the alley behind my boardinghouse, he
took out his guitar, serenaded me with 'Walking the Floor Over
You.' He sounded like Ernest Tubb. I hated country music! I
slammed the window, yanked the shade—but I was too late."

I pictured my grandfather's hands, cracked in the winter,
smeared with pine-sap, ash, and drops of oils from his traps.
When he was young, he skinned small animals, and scraped off
the gristle and fat, and nailed the hides to planks.

"Did you and he both think about not showing up for your
wedding?" I said.

"It was raining that day," my grandmother said, laughing.
"He had some repairs he wanted to finish. At the time, he was
hauling coal, driving a dump truck. It wasn't steady work."

My younger son says that he wants to be a worker-man and
a Caesar salad chef. He gathers daisy-like weeds wherever

he goes—the playground, the greenway, the overgrazed field behind our house. Sometimes, he ignores the sliding board and the yellow climbing tunnels, collects fallen leaves instead. He loves to play with old cardboard boxes. These he climbs in, builds with, tears into pieces.

At the museum, he goes to the fun factory on the roof, stands at the bubble tank and blows bubbles. He dips both hands into the sudsy liquid, then his forearms. I know he's thinking about jumping in; I've seen him eat from a snow drift face-first, seen him lie down in a puddle, move his arms and legs back and forth. He's a believer in total immersion.

In the half bath, my wife changes a bulb. "Want help," the boy says. "I help you." He shuts and opens the door, shuts and opens it again. He makes dark, he makes light.

From the boy, I am learning another way to see.

At sunset, I walk to the top of the knob, the zenith and center of my grandparents' farm. I can begin here. I look in all directions, try to take in the acres they mowed, the rust-roofed sheds and pale silo, the diminishing pond in deep shadow.

I try to bring back as much of them as I can. For me, for my sons. I am thinking about the burning planet they will live on.

Once, I stood with my grandfather on the knob. He pointed his hand and named the adjacent counties. Maybe he also said Texas Mountain, Pifer Mountain, and Laurel, Limestone, Polecat, the long folded ridges, the edge of the Alleghenies. Maybe he thought about the starving Confederate soldiers on Laurel Mountain, who had surrendered for a wagon of hard bread. The ridges bounded us, as if we were looking out from the middle of a fancy bowl, scalloped and hazy blue, or perhaps the line of mountains was gray-green, the color of pond water.

That was before the windfarm was built on Laurel, before

sixty-one turbines and batteries in steel boxes were installed, before their red blinkers flashed warnings every night. Before cow burps were linked to greenhouse gas, glacial melt. Before the first coyotes came from out-of-state and threatened livestock.

Once, my grandfather baled hay, strung barbed wire, dug fence holes, clipped bull calves. I think his work was a strain of love.

Once, a sinkhole opened in the meadow where the cattle grazed. My grandfather told me some settler a hundred years back had mined part of the farm. I thought about a man who had crawled into the earth, pushing a wheelbarrow ahead of him. I thought about unseen cavities lacing my grandfather's fields, tunnels where the long-ago miner had dug out the coal, leaving behind an understory.

I helped my grandfather fill the bed of his pickup with stones from creeks in the woods. Before we dropped the stones into the hole, he let me have a look.

On my hands and knees, face in a ring of earth, I peered in, and felt, or almost felt, a draft, a cool shivery gust that smelled like ashes and old leaves. I took in an impossible underground room, black and jagged, shiny and unlit.

My wife gives the older boy a toy chainsaw for Easter. When I park in our driveway near the Leyland cypresses, he surprises me: he gleefully blurts, "Cut down wild trees," and his glee spreads to me: I cheer for him. I think, that was a four-word sentence (his slow acquisition has me counting every word). And then I think, let him be saw-delighted, machine-delighted, but maybe we can also teach him to be curious about trees, to care about nature.

I take the boy to Red Clay State Park, fifteen miles from our house: *last seat of Cherokee national government*, according to the park website, *where the Trail of Tears began in 1838, where the Cherokee learned they had lost their mountains, streams, and valleys.* We walk through the powwow grounds, where the Cherokee women sang their old songs last summer. As we hike the Council of Trees Trail, the boy stops and examines sticks, rocks, fallen logs. We climb Suits Hill, pass under maples and black gums. I carry him part of the way.

At the Blue Hole, in the shade of sourwoods, we look at water that's the blue of twilight, the blue of slate. We cool our feet in the outflow, then share a Gala apple. The boy offers me the core. "You like bones," he says.

My grandmother rode with me to the department store, bought a new dress shirt for my grandfather. He would have it, along with his gray slacks and bus driving shoes, to wear when he slept in the earth.

At his funeral, standing near him in the long box, she greeted each mourner, gave each a glance, a word, a nod, then turned her eyes back to him. Once, she said, "He looks good in that shade of blue. "

A relative corrected her: "He's not really here," meaning only the spirit has ceaseless life.

She replied, "Yes, but I love what's still here."

Our family wouldn't listen to his song tapes or look at pictures of him, waiting until danger of missing him too much had passed.

For forty years, my grandmother and my grandfather were farmers on Pea Ridge. Each morning, she walked out to see the cows. When a new calf couldn't get started on his mother, she held the nursing bucket for him.

For fifteen years, she has gardened alone.

Come spring, she will look for trout lily and trillium in the ravine. Will crumble soil with her arthritic fingers. Will make two gardens. Will mix Miracle-Gro granules. Will freeze snap peas so that she can taste springtime when she thaws them in January.

Come fall, she will try to fill a big sinkhole in the back yard. She will move gravel, haul loads of rocks from the garden in her cart, get some extra shale and shovel it in for two hours. When it still isn't filled, she will cover it over with boards.

She will cut out potato eyes, and hang shiny pie pans and strips of foil to protect her gardens from crows, and put together extension cords so that she can set a radio among the tomato plants, play rock music all night to scare away the deer.

When she can no longer walk to the bird feeders hung in the peach trees, she will leave little piles of millet and sunflower seed on the porch rails.

This might be the last time the older boy and I see my grandmother. He's four-and-a-half. She's still living on her farm. She's ninety-three, sits near a TV tray, plastic cup, drinking straw. She and the boy kick a cloth ball, play keep-away. She's mostly quiet. She's unsure of her words.

I don't know what to say.

On the day we get back to Tennessee, the boy takes out crayons and construction paper. While he draws, I read to him the parts of this story about my grandparents and their farm. When I finish, he says he doesn't like it. I ask him how I can make it better. He says, "Put in what Grandma looks like." Then he draws two big turquoise circles. He says, "These are dream-ponds. They help you go to sleep."

That night, I tuck him in, then his younger brother. I'm tired from the long drive. One boy is quiet. One boy chatters for a while, and then he sleeps too. My wife is working the night shift at a psychiatric hospital. Our house is moon-silvered, a deep ocean, the holdfast of a dreaming family. My life depends on theirs. We repeat. We are connected. There's laurel dace in me, Angus cow in me, hickory tree, amber seaweed. I listen for faint cries, bits of story.

Acknowledgments

Thank you to the publications in which these stories previously appeared.

> *Appalachian Review*: "Daughter with a Star on Her Brow"
> *Baltimore Review*: "Fire Season"
> *Best Small Fictions 2017*: "What the Beech Tree Knows"
> *Change Seven*: "In the Hollow"
> *The Citron Review*: "Bad Blood"
> *EPOCH*: "June Drop"
> *Indiana Review* and *Barren Magazine*: "Ring of Earth"
> *Michigan Quarterly Review*: "The Algebra of Longing"
> *New Ohio Review*: "Crow Stories" and "Wax Museum"
> *Ninth Letter*: "Sons with Apples in Their Hands"
> *Salamander*: "Velvet Knob"
> *Still: the Journal*: "The Sinks of Gandy"
> *Tahoma Literary Review*: "What the Beech Tree Knows"
> *Tin House*: "The Labor of Her Hands"
> *Western Humanities Review*: "Bad Blood"
> *Witness*: "Only the Wind"

While I was revising, Laura Long and Natalie Sypolt generously shared with me wisdom, vision, and hope—invaluable gifts that helped me finish this book. A special thank you to both of them.

I'm also grateful to many other writers whose words and lives have guided me again and again—especially TJ Beitelman, Kelly Magee, Michelle Ross, Jacinda Townsend, Harriette Simpson Arnow, Jenn Blair, Annette Saunooke Clapsaddle, Rebecca Harding Davis, Louise Erdrich, Denise Giardina, Cathryn Hankla, Charlotte Holmes, Denton Loving, Irene McKinney, Lucien Darjeun Meadows, Laura Leigh Morris, Julie Otsuka, Ann Pancake, Mary Lee Settle, Anne Spencer, Ida Stewart, Susan O'Dell Underwood, Jessie van Eerden, and Marianne Worthington.

About the Author

William Woolfitt's fiction chapbook, *The Boy with Fire in His Mouth* (2014), won the Epiphany Editions contest judged by Darin Strauss. He has also written several books of poems, including *Spring Up Everlasting* (Mercer University Press, 2020). His short stories and essays have been published in *Tin House*, *Best Small Fictions*, *The Cincinnati Review*, *Appalachian Review*, *Epoch*, *Michigan Quarterly Review*, and elsewhere. After growing up in West Virginia, Woolfitt relocated to another part of Appalachia—Cleveland, Tennessee, where he lives with his family and teaches college writing classes.